SLEEP
MY DEAR

GODS NEVER FEEL LONELINESS

Maryse Marullo

ABOUT THE AUTHOR

Step into the world of Maryse Marullo, which explores the haunting beauty of love in the shadows. Hailing from the landscapes of Canada. Maryse is an author who thrives on the edges of passion and darkness, crafting narratives that delve into the depths of the human heart. She's an addict for dark, taboo, and forbidden romance.

Follow her on socials for updates on upcoming releases and a glimpse into the mind behind the captivating tales of dark romance.

https://beacons.ai/authormarysemarullo

iv – SLEEP MY DEAR

DEDICATION

For the lovers.
For the loners.
For the dreamers.
And the vengeful badass out there.

(There's a surprise at the end)

x – SLEEP MY DEAR

ACKNOWLEDGMENTS

Thanks to my amazing, intelligent, and creative children. You helped me so much with the worldbuilding of this book. You are the best. I love you, Mama xoxo

Thank you to my man, for enduring me speak about my stories and ideas day and night.

Rosalyn Butler, Tara MacNeil, Lauren MacIsaac, for always being by my side. Love you.

PLAYLIST

The weekend – One of the girls
Amber Run - Worship
The Neighborhood – Daddy issues
Ruelle – War of hearts
Tommee Profitt, Brooke – I can't help falling in love
2WEI – Toxic
Ursine Vulpine – Wicked Game
Taylor Swift – Don't blame me
Unsecret ft. Krigare – Vendetta
Unsecret ft. Nicole Serrano – Coming for you
Elley duhé – In the middle of the night

CONTENT WARNING

For adults only

This is a dark romantasy

The content of this book may be triggering and disturbing to some readers. This is a dark romantasy. Please take a warning that the content is for adults only.

If you're uncomfortable with dark, don't read this book.

It's a dark romance with trauma, nightmares, possessives, and morally grey characters.

Several sexual and topics aspects of the book can be disturbing for some people. The subjects include the following, but are not limited to:

Betrayal

BDSM

Blood play

Death

Dragon

Dual-POV

Gore

Gods

Kidnapping

Lies

Manipulation

Mature language

Murder

Orgy

Panic attack

Praise

Possession

Primal play

PTSD

Trauma

Violence

Voyeurisme

17 – SLEEP MY DEAR

Chapter 1

Aurora

)———◇◇◇———(

"I feel like staying home," I murmur to my reflection.

The sunlight peeking through my beloved rainbow-tainted bathroom windows fills the room with warmth and colors. The shades of pink, yellow, blue, and even green make me smile.

Usually, I don't have any trouble waking up and going to work. I love my job as a pastry chef. But I have a strange feeling today. It's as if I would be better off staying indoors.

I quickly wash my face in the sink, add a little bit of mascara, and put on my favorite apron, the yellow one with little cupcakes patterned all over it. It always brings joy to client's faces.

And if there's one thing I know how to do well, it's making people feel comfortable and happy.

I step down the stairs of my little house and head to the kitchen, the aroma of freshly brewed coffee fills the air, and I'm so damn grateful to have used a portion of my savings to buy this coffee machine, the automatic timer saved my life a couple of mornings.

Humming a tune, I braid my hair with practiced ease, glancing at my reflection in the microwave glass. A sweet smile on my face, but if you look closely, you might see a touch of sadness in my eyes.

Crafting masks is an art I have mastered – kindness and humor blended seamlessly to shield deeper emotions.

I hate feeling.

After I lock the door using my keys, I step out into the bright sunlight of the Vermont woods. The quiet streets welcome me, like every day since I'm eighteen years old.

The trees whisper in the wind, their leaves sounding like a soothing song. I enjoy my stroll from home to downtown, which takes about fifteen minutes.

It's something I do every day to help burn off the extra calories from the snacks I eat while I'm working.

I could have bought a car when I came to live here, but I quickly realized that in this small town, I only needed my legs and a bit of determination to get everywhere.

I turn the corner of my quiet street and step onto the sidewalk of the principal road. The streets welcome me with a lively buzz. The soft breeze carries the scent of blooming flowers, and the sound of laughter echoes from nearby cafes. I meander along the sidewalk, passing by quaint storefronts adorned with vibrant displays. Each step reveals a new delight – the sight of children playing in the fountain, the sound of a street musician's guitar strumming, and the taste of freshly baked pastries wafting from the bakery on the corner. It's a picture-perfect scene.

I look straight ahead and see my destination; the wall facing the street is all glass, decorated with paintings Meya takes care to refresh each season. As summer begins, she embellishes it with tulips, sunflowers, and all sorts of lovely wildflowers.

The bakery stood at the heart of the town and it's one of the most well-known and beloved gathering spots for everyone.

I enter, and regulars greet me with smiles. *God, I love this place*. "Hello, Aurora." Mrs. Langford crooned.

I make my way behind the glass counter, the display showcases an array of delights – cupcakes with rainbow sprinkles, golden croissants, and cookies that look like miniature pieces of art.

I enter the little kitchen at the back, ready to whip up some magic with flour and sugar.

I'm measuring ingredients, making sure everything is just right. Meya, the owner of the bakery, and my best friend enter. "Morning, sunshine!"

"Hey there. Ready for another day of turning flour into happiness?" I reply, looking up from the bowl before me.

"Always! What's your masterpiece for today?" Meya asks, grabbing an espresso cup on the shelf.

"How about some raspberry-filled pastries? They're like little pockets of flavors," I suggest, my fingers dancing over the recipe cards. "And I've never made them."

"Perfect! Let's make the town's taste buds dance. Oh, did you hear about Old Mr. Jenkins trying to do the moonwalk at the town square yesterday?" Meya shares with a grin.

I burst into laughter. "No way! How did that turn out?"

Meya attempts a moonwalk, and we both crack up. "Let's just say the town got a free comedy show. He's got moves for an old pal. I'll give him that."

I giggle and roll my eyes. "He could have broken his hips," I add.

She playfully nudged me and said, "You know, your laugh always makes my days brighter."

I shrug with a sweet smile. "Maybe it's just easier to sprinkle a little happiness on others when you're trying to find some for yourself."

Meya gives me a knowing look, a silent understanding between friends. "Well, you're doing a mighty fine job, my friend."

In the busy commotion of the day, memories of the car accident unexpectedly come rushing back to me. I can hear the tires screeching and the waves crashing in my mind, and I feel the same fear of the ocean overwhelming me all over again.

I take a deep breath, trying to shake off the memories and focus on the comforting scent of raspberries and whipped cream.

Stop thinking about them.

Chapter 2

Aurora

The bakery is winding down, and I stand at the sink, gently washing the coffee cups and plates. The warm water feels soothing on my hands.

Meya saunters in with her usual energy. "Hey, blondie! Just kick out the last customer, all in good spirits, of course." She grimaces.

I chuckle, glancing at her. "You have a way with people."

Meya grin, her hazel eyes twinkling.

I continue washing the dishes, and she leans on the counter. "You know, I know when something is off with your pretty ass."

There is a brief pause as the water runs, and I can't help but sigh. "Sometimes, it feels like I'm trying to bake happiness for everyone else, but I'm missing the recipe for myself."

Meya's expression softened. "Wow. This was cringe of you to say. But I get it. You went through so much. But you're not alone, Aurora."

I nod, grateful for her understanding. "Thanks, It means a lot."

She bumps my shoulder playfully. "Did you still get nightmares?"

Her question gives me the creeps and my heart stops for a beat. "Every night. I'm so sick of it, I can't sleep."

"Did you speak about it with Doctor Phills?" She asks, concern.

"Yes, but he wanted to put me on some medication. I didn't want it. Now, enough of the heavy stuff. Let's finish up and grab some dinner. How about we try that new place downtown?"

She smiles, she knows I hate to talk about my past, and my nightmares. "Sounds like a plan. Lead the way, my friend."

The sun bathes the streets in a warm glow as we lock the door, the click echoing through the emptying town. Usually, at five pm, people are in one of the three restaurants or, at home.

We stroll down the charming streets, passing quaint shops and exchanging greetings with familiar faces.

"So, spill the beans, girl," Meya teased. "Any handsome guys caught your eye lately?"

I chuckle, feeling the blush creep onto my cheeks. "You know me, Meya. I'm too busy with you and sugar to notice anyone."

Meya rolls or eyes and sighs loudly. "Come on, there must be someone who's got your heart doing the tango. Or maybe an occasional dick?"

I explode in a laugh. "My vibrator does the job and shut up."

Meya's expression softens, and she gives my hand a reassuring squeeze. "Love can be a tricky bitch, my friend."

We arrive at the new restaurant and enter between two large wooden and glass doors. The air hummed with laughter, the clinking of glasses, and the aroma of steak well done. We found a cozy corner and settled in.

Over delicious cocktails, we continued our heart-to-heart. Meya told me about her funny love stories, and we laughed together. Her last one-night stand, who threw up on her hair while she was giving him a head.

What a luck. I almost lose consciousness while laughing so hard.

Meya grinned mischievously, sipping her cocktail. "Aurora, look at our server. He's like a handsome mystery that just walked into our small town. I smell romance in the air."

I giggle, scanning the room. A tall, dark-haired man with a smile as warm as the summer sun, caught my eyes. "He does stand out. Must be new around here."

Meya dances her shoulder playfully. "Well, girl, it's time for you to unleash your charm."

I chuckle. "Oh, Meya, you, and your matchmaking schemes. But hey, why not?" I straighten my back, trying to muster some courage, but I think the big glasses of sangria I just drank in less than a minute are already catching on me. *Fuck me.*

Our server approached and I smiled warmly. "Hi there! I'm Aurora, and this is Meya. We're on a mission to discover the wonders of this new place. What do you recommend?"

The server's brown eyes sparkled, and he introduced himself as Josh. "Welcome! The special tonight is fantastic. The chef's recommendation is the grilled salmon, and we have a refreshing peach-mint cocktail. What do you think?"

My best friend looks at me, giving an encouraging look.

"I say we go for it! Josh, we'll take two of those peach-mint delights and the grilled salmon." I speak.

Josh laughs, "Coming right up! You two seem like a lot of fun."

As he walks away, Meya wink at me. "See? Engaging in some good old-fashioned charm. You're a natural, Aurora!"

We had a nice evening with delicious food and lots of peach-mint cocktails. Josh came over to talk and stop with us while he served other tables.

He told us about his trip to our town and why he liked its simple charm. He looked strong as he moved around the tables easily, and his short black hair added to his charm.

But the night comes to an end when he picks up our plates and mentions returning with our bills. Meya leans on the table and fixes her glossy little affected eyes on mine. "Aurora, I've got an idea. Why not invite Josh back to your place for a last drink? I f you know what I mean." She murmurs, moving her arms like she's fucking the air.

Giggling, I consider the idea. But before I could gather the courage, Josh approaches with a panties-dropper grin. "Here's your bills, but before paying would you like a dessert or perhaps another round of cocktails?"

Meya seizes the opportunity and chimes in, "Actually, we are thinking of wrapping up the night. But Aurora here," she nudges me with a finger and a mischievous glint, "is contemplating some home comforts. You know, a nightcap in the coziness of her own space."

Josh's eyes dance between mine and hers when finally lands his gaze on me. "That sounds like a lovely idea. If you're up for it, Aurora, I'd be happy to drop you. I just finished my shift, so I'm all yours."

Blushing, I nod, the warmth of the cocktails making me bolder than usual. "Sure, I'd like that."

Meya stands up with a playful smirk. "Well, I'll leave you two to enjoy the rest of the night. Aurora, consider this my treat. You are on vacation tomorrow. Josh, take good care of our sweet friend here."

She winks at me, and with a quick hug, she left the resto-bar, leaving Josh and me in a momentary silence.

He broke the ice with a chuckle. "Your friend is a character. So, shall we head to your place for that drink?"

"Yeah, let's go. It's just a short walk from here." I agree.

Chapter 3

Aurora

We walk through the darkened streets, the summer night surrounding us with its tranquility. The stars above flicker like distant fireflies, and a gentle breeze rustles the leaves of the trees.

Josh breaks the silence, "So, Aurora, tell me more about yourself. What's your story?"

I hesitate for a moment, the courage boosted by the night and perhaps a bit of the evening's cocktails, I breathe and just go for it. "Well, it's a bit of a long story. But, hey, let's make the walk interesting."

With a gentle chuckle, he nods. "I'm all ears. Share as much as you want."

"I'm an orphan. I lost my whole family in a car accident when I was twelve. It's... it's tough, you know? After that, I got tossed around in the system, moving from one not-so-great family to another. It feels like I'm never really home."

Josh's eyes soften, sadness and surprise in his gaze. "That sounds incredibly difficult, Aurora. I can't even imagine."

"Yeah," I continue, my gaze fixed on the path ahead. "It took until I turned eighteen to finally decide I've had enough. I packed my bags, left the system, and set out on my own. I end up here in this little town."

The beautiful man listens to me attentively, his presence a comforting anchor. "And the bakery?" he asks.

I grin, this is a memory I don't mind bringing back. "Well, when I arrived, I needed a job. Meya was just opening this bakery, and we connected. It's been my haven ever since. Baking, the town, it all just clicks."

We reach my doorstep, and the porch light flickers to life. I turn to Josh, gratitude in my eyes. "Thanks for listening. Not everyone bothers to hear the whole story."

He smiles, genuine and kind. "Aurora, I'm glad you shared about you. Sometimes, it's good to let the stories out."

"Come on in! Make yourself at home," I say, my voice all sweetness.

Inside, the vibrant decor screams happiness, my way of filling this space with all the good I can.

I turn to him, eyes twinkling, "Want something to drink? Tea, coffee, or something a bit more fun?"

"Cocktail would be good." He smiles.

"Tell me about you," I demand.

"Ah, nothing special. I came to settle here as you know, sort of by chance. I took this job at the restaurant, and I like the atmosphere, so I'm staying here, for now. I must admit that I was seeing someone, but she lives very far away and... she doesn't always take care of me. So..."

On my way to the kitchen, I catch my reflection in my pink mirror on the wall, doubt creeps in. Confidence slips away. *Someone.*

I still get out glasses and the ingredients for a cocktail. But my hopes to replace my vibrator tonight, are gone now.

The ice clinks in the glasses as I skillfully mix our drinks, and I feel Josh's presence behind me, his body pressing gently against mine.

The air crackles with a weird energy. "You're quite the mixologist," he murmurs, his breath tickling my ear.

Turning to face him, I extend a glass in his direction and step back, our fingers brushing in the exchange.

Raising my own, I offer a toast, "To unexpected meet. And new friends."

Fuck I hope he catches the message.

I take a slow sip of my drink, the cool liquid dancing on my tongue. The atmosphere is charged, the air thick with discomfort. Josh's hazel gaze intensifies, locking onto mine with an intensity that sends a goosebump down my spine. He places his glass delicately on the table.

Suddenly, his hand wraps around the nape of my neck, pulling me towards him. I feel the warmth of his breath on my lips as he tries to bring our mouths together. It's a bold move, and for a moment, I think I want it. But now, with his lips so close, uncertainty floods my senses.

I can't do that.

In a split-second decision, I back away, creating a bit of distance. "Excuse me," I mutter, the words catching in my throat.

I can feel the weight of his eyes, and a mixture of confusion and fear swirls within me.

Fuck, fuck, fuck.

He's fueled by frustration or perhaps a wounded ego, it shows in the way his posture is now rigid.

He slams his fist onto the table, the sound cutting through the silence of the room. "What the hell, you fucking cocktease?" He snaps, his tone full of anger.

"Look, I thought I wanted this, but I need a moment to think. Can we just... take a step back?"

He scoffs, his irritation palpable. "Take a step back? You were practically begging for it a minute ago!"

Ok, he's taking this too far.

I feel a simmering frustration bubbling in me, and my voice steadies as I stand my ground. "People change their minds, Josh. It's not a crime. I just need some space right now."

His frustration transforms into rage, his voice raising, "Space? We were having a good time, and now you're pulling this shit. You're such a tease!"

I take a deep breath, steadying myself. "I'm not a tease. I just need some time to figure things out. It's not about you."

He steps closer, his fury escalating. "Not about me? You're leading me on, and now you're playing the victim? Pathetic!"

My patience wears thin. I'm a nice and polite person, but deep down, I still am the woman trapped in a traumatic and sad past who needed to defend herself.

"Josh, I won't be spoken to like that. If you can't respect my boundaries, then maybe it's best if you just fuck off."

The words hang in the air, and a tense silence follows. The room seems to be still.

I hold his gaze, unyielding, my resolve cutting through the tension. The ball is in his court now, and I wait to see how he'll react.

Josh storms off, leaving me standing there, feeling relief and frustration at the same time.

I lock the door behind him, the click signaling the end of this turbulent night. And the chance to sleep with him one day.

A heavy sigh escapes me as I walk up the stairs, the weight of the end of the night lingering in my mind.

I don't want love.

Once inside my room, I peel off my clothes, shedding the tension along with them. The cool air of the room brushes against my skin, providing a welcome contrast to the heat of the previous moment.

I head to the bathroom, my routine a familiar anchor, A safe place after the strong feelings that happened.

The soft glow of the bathroom light envelops me, casting a gentle warmth on the grey-tiled floor.

I stand before the sink, brushing my teeth, and with a deep breath, I spit into it and step into the shower. The water, at just the right temperature, fucking boiling, cascades over my body like a gentle waterfall.

The sensation is both cleansing and renewing, a ritual of self-care that allows me to emerge from the shower feeling lighter, both in spirit and body.

"I knew I should have stayed home today," I grumble. I turn off the water, droplets cling to my skin like tiny diamonds. I grab the fluffy towel hanging nearby and wrap it around me, the soft fabric comforting against my damp skin.

With a contented sigh, I leave the bathroom and walk directly into my bedroom.

I'm so tired.

But I don't want to fall asleep, because I know, I'll have nightmares.

It's been a year of dark dreams, fear, and sadness each time I close my eyes, and I don't want that anymore. I just want a *fucking* night of peaceful sleep.

I slip between the soft sheets, grab my phone on the nightstand, and send a quick text to Meya.

Me: I'm home, alive, and well. Talk to you tomorrow.

It's a simple message, but it will do the job.

The night may have taken an unexpected turn, but it's nothing to what waits for me.

Waves.

Water.

Chapter 4

Aurora

I find myself standing on this tiny, coarse beach, facing a massive ocean with waves that roar like thunder. The sand beneath my feet feels rough and unforgiving, contrasting sharply with the vastness of the water in front of me.

The atmosphere is heavy, with a dark sky and an eerie feeling in the air. The waves are colossal, rising and crashing with an intimidating force that seems to mirror the chaos in my mind.

The air is filled with the scent of salt, carried by the persistent breeze that wraps around me. There's no sun, the sky is a canvas of deep indigos and grays, intensifying the feeling of foreboding.

This small stretch of beach is like a fragile line of defense against the might of the ocean.

In this desolate place, I stand alone, confronted by the relentless power of nature. Panic tightens its grip on my chest, constricting my breath with each crashing wave.

No, no no.

The wind howls through my tangled hair and cries in the distance, distant pleas for help. Each scream is a discordant note.

My thoughts race, colliding with each other. I feel like the ocean is angry, and the waves are trying to swallow everything in their path.

In an attempt to find some solace, I close my eyes, hoping to shut out the overwhelming sights and sounds. It's a nightmare, it's a nightmare.

Wake up, wake up.

However, even in the darkness behind my eyelids, the fear persists.

The transition is sudden, and before I fully comprehend it, the familiar ground beneath my feet disappears.

The relentless pull of panic has become a physical force, and I find myself submerged in the dark, vast expanse of the ocean. The waves, once observed from the safety of the shore, now surround me, their power overwhelming.

The water is cold, and it engulfs me with a chilling embrace. Panic tightens its grip, a relentless companion in this new, disorienting realm. I can feel the weight of the ocean pressing against me.

In this unfamiliar darkness, the cries for help, now muffled by the water, take on an eerie quality. They reverberate through the ocean, creating a haunting symphony that intensifies the sense of fear.

I kick my legs, attempting to propel myself towards the surface, but the water feels like an unyielding barrier.

WAKE UP AURORA, WAKE UP.

The waves, once observed from a distance, now tower above me, casting ominous shadows that play tricks on my imagination.

Every stroke feels like a desperate attempt to regain control, but the dark water resists, closing in around me.

The ocean becomes an abyss, swallowing both sound and sight. It's a lonely, frightening place, and the panic that accompanies me is an unwelcome companion, echoing through the water like a silent scream.

I struggle against the currents, yearning for the solidity of the shore, the familiarity of the beach. The panic, now intertwined with the water that surrounds me, creates a surreal and terrifying experience.

The weight of the ocean presses against my chest, making each breath a struggle. It's not just the water; it's the fear that engulfs me. As I attempt to swim towards the surface, the water resists, indifferent to my desperate struggle.

It's an overwhelming force, a reminder of my powerlessness in the face of nature's might.

Drowning is not just a physical experience; it's a visceral awareness of the imminent threat, a realization that every gasp for air brings me no closer to survival.

The darkness deepens as I sink further, the pressure building and the water becoming an inescapable shroud.

The panic intensifies, morphing into a silent scream that echoes in the underwater silence. Each passing moment feels like an eternity, a cruel suspension between life and death.

The water wraps around me, and it feels like it's filling up my lungs. It hurts—a sharp, heavy pain. No matter how hard I try, I can't get to the surface. It's like the ocean doesn't care.

I decide to stop fighting.

A thought creeps in, maybe I never deserved to live anyway. It's a sad feeling, and I start to let go.

Everything gets blurry, and slowly, I drift into unconsciousness.

Chapter 5

Aurora

)————◇◇◇————(

I open my eyes, and everything is wet.

My clothes, my hair, even the ground I'm lying on. I try to cough, but it's like water is stuck in my throat. It's not a good feeling.

I'm on my tummy, and the ground feels weird, not like my bed at home. It's not soft or warm. It's hard and makes me feel uncomfortable.

I push myself up from the cold, dirt floor. It sends shivers through me. Looking around, all I see is trees. Big, tall trees that seem to touch the sky. A vast forest, it's like it goes on forever.

The air feels strange, something is not right. It's not sunny or bright; it's dark and eerie. The sky is green and grey, full of clouds like it's going to rain, but it's not raining.

There's just this heavy feeling in the air. The silence is everywhere even the birds forgot to chirp. It's so quiet that it feels like the whole world is holding its breath.

I straighten up, dizzy and shivering, my clothes sticking to me. The ground squishes under my shoes.

I take a step, and it's like I'm walking on a sponge.

"Hello?"

"Is there anyone?" my voice gets lost in the quiet.

I start walking, trying to find a way out of this weird place.

Where the heck am I?

The trees seem to watch me, their branches like long fingers reaching out.

Wake up Aurora.

I wrap my arms around myself, trying to ward off the cold that's seeping into my bones. My whole-body shakes, and my teeth chatter together like tiny percussion instruments.

I give myself a little pinch, hoping it's all just another nightmare. But instead of waking up, all I get is a sharp "ouch."

The dampness clings to my skin, and the forest feels like it's closing in on me.

I take another step on the squishy ground, making weird noises with each footfall.

In front of me, as if summoned by some unseen force, a path starts to appear in the woods. And I stop walking, gasping at it. "What the hell…"

The trees are making way for me, revealing a trail on the dirt and moss-covered ground.

It's not a clear road, but it's something to follow.

I decide to trust it and start walking along the path. The damp leaves and twigs crackle under my shoes. Everything casts strange shadows that dance around me. I can hear odd sounds if I listen closely – distant cries, haunting moans.

Not the kind of noises that bring comfort.

I tighten my grip on myself and quicken my pace. The path unfolds before me like a silent guide through the mysterious woods.

I keep my ears tuned to the strange sounds; each step accompanied by an unsettling symphony.

I can't shake the feeling that I'm not alone, that something unseen is watching me from the thick green fog.

Yet, I follow the path, hoping it will lead me out of this eerie silence and into answers.

I'm walking, walking, and walking. I feel like it's been hours of walking. The ground is still wet and... *what the hell*, moving? it's breathing?

Suddenly, I catch a reflection in the corner of my eyes, there are green lights. I focus my eyes on the moving speck, it's fireflies, all around.

They're not the usual kind, though. They shine a bright green and make the air look even more magical.

The lights float and twinkle, and I smile at them. "Hey, little buddy."

One of them flies in front of my nose and touches it softly, making me giggle. "You're not so scary."

I stop walking not to scare the little bug, but the damn trees start making strange sounds again –cries and moans.

I reach out to touch my new friend, but it flies just out of my grasp. Its ghostly glow feels warm on my hand. Like it's an ember.

"I would love for you to bring your friends over here, I'm so cold." I joke to the tiny light.

I shiver and start walking again on the path, continuing to watch the fireflies shine between the trees.

But I jump when a handful of them come up to my height, flying in circles around my body.

Did they hear me?

"Oh wow, thank you..." I murmur.

I'm going crazy.

I keep going, following the lights and the path deeper into the forest.

After walking for what feels like forever, I finally reach the end of the forest. In front of me is a big open space with a huge stone bridge stretching across it.

WOW, it's humongous.

The wind is super strong, pushing and pulling at me. It's tugging on my clothes and making my hair fly all over the place.

Above, crows are yelling in the green and grey sky.

Their voices mix with the howling wind, creating a spooky symphony.

I tense, feeling a bit alone and small in this vast open space.

I stop walking right at the beginning of the bridge, it's narrow, and there's nothing to hold onto on the sides. I'm scared that the wind might blow me off.

I take a deep breath and step onto the bridge, trying to keep my balance.

The wind pushes against me, making it hard to walk straight.

On the other side of the bridge, there's something that catches my eye. It looks like a castle, but not just any castle – a small but tall one on what seems to be a little hill on a floating piece of forest.

Dark and mysterious, with a central tower that reaches up to the sky. It's both scary and fascinating.

Its black color does nothing to ease my nerves.

I continue across the narrow bridge, the wind pushes me and I lose my balance. A haunting scream escapes my lips and I crouch on the cold stones of the bridge.

Holy hell.

My breath is short, and my heart pounds in my neck like the blood flow wants to escape my veins.

I look above me at the sky for a minute and try to calm myself. "You will not fall. You're in a dream," I reassure myself.

I take the biggest breath I've ever taken, use my hands in front of me to push myself up again and direct my gaze in front of me.

"You will not fear," I tell myself.

Chapter 6

Aurora

I did it.

I crossed this huge stone bridge, and damn, it feels like an accomplishment.

But the real relief hit me when my feet touched the dirt on the other side.

I dare to look down, and there it is – this massive, endless void. Black, thick, like it could go on forever.

I sit on a strong log, taking a breather. I need this time to sort out my thoughts and emotions.

Looking around. This forest isn't as thick as the one on the other side of that scary bridge.

Now, the trees don't seem as creepy. They're just normal trees with green leaves, and there are even white flowers scattered on the ground.

The air, which felt heavy before, seems to get a bit lighter now.

Taking a deep breath, I inspect my clothes, realizing I haven't seen them before. "What the heck."

During the earlier panic, it slipped my mind, and I didn't notice.

They're dry now, *thankfully*.

A pair of black jeans and a crisp white button-up loose shirt.

No bra underneath, which adds a surprising twist. It's odd how little details escape your attention when you're catching your breath and trying not to die.

I heave a sigh and pull myself up, setting off toward the castle. The crows above me circled in the sky and squawked like they've got a bone to pick.

I shoot them a defiant middle finger and keep walking.

Screw them.

I just want to wake up.

The castle looms closer, only a few steps away from the log I was sitting on. I can't help but gasp. It's stunning.

The entire structure is black, but it's not just black – it's the kind of black that eats up the light, mysterious and alluring.

Every edge seems to tell a story, intricate carvings revealing themselves in the stone. It's a breathtaking sight, and for a moment, the chaos of the crows fades away in the face of this beautiful, eerie castle.

Each brick seems to hold secrets, etched with the weight of centuries.

I feel like an intruder– which I am, and the urgency to remain unnoticed intensifies with every cautious step.

"Wow." I mutter.

I approach the doorstep, my eyes fixating on the colossal door before me.

Its sheer size is intimidating, an imposing guardian to whatever lies beyond. The black wood is weathered, and the carvings etched into its surface are nothing short of disturbing.

Oh my god.

It's full of faces, faces twisted and contorted. Some appear to be locked in perpetual cries of pain, while others wear expressions of profound fear.

Monsters, grotesque and nightmarish, intertwine with the human forms, creating a surreal art I've never seen before, that chills my blood.

Despite the unease settling in my stomach, curiosity compels me forward.

The craftsmanship, though disturbing, radiates an unusual charm drawing me closer like a moth to a flame. "It's so realistic," I murmur to myself.

Standing just inches away, I take in the intricate carvings. The texture of the wood is rough beneath my fingertips. I can almost feel the emotions emanating from the faces and creatures.

It's as if the door itself holds the memories of the faces on it. A hesitant breath escapes my lips as I prepare to push the door open.

"It's because they're real, my dear."

His voice hits me like a wave, a deep, resonant sound that's both manly and beautiful.

I freeze, my heart pounding.

I turn rapidly before me stands a man of unearthly beauty, a mixture of strength and grace. His frame is tall and muscular, yet thin, a walking paradox.

His short hair, as white as snow, and his eyes, a mesmerizing silver-blue, seem to pierce through the very fabric of my being.

And I don't have a bra!

"Excuse me," I stammer, my voice carrying confusion, shyness, and fear.

"Where am I?" The frantic words spill from my lips as I try to make sense of this surreal encounter.

Instinctively, I hug myself on the chest, trying to cover my nipple peeking through this damn white shirt.

He just stands there, his eyes dancing where my breaths were seconds ago, with a subtle smile playing on his lips. It's so soft you could almost miss it, but the dimples at the corners of his mouth give him away.

"Welcome," he finally speaks, his voice like a velvet caress. "You find yourself in fucking nightmares, darling. Literally."

My eyes widen, and my mind races to comprehend his words. "So, I'm dreaming?" I feel the panic rising in my voice.

He chuckles, the sound melodic yet tinged with something I can't quite place. Perhaps it's *fuck boy* attitude.

"Not anymore."

I glance around, trying to grasp my surroundings, but everything seems to blur. "What? Why am I here? How did I get here?" I fire off questions in a desperate attempt to make sense of the situation.

His smile deepens, and he takes a step closer. "All in good time, my dear. The answers will reveal themselves when the time is right." His silver-blue eyes hold wisdom beyond their years, and I can't help but feel a mix of comfort and unease.

I take a step back, my eyes never leaving his. "I need to go back. I have a life, people waiting for me." His smile remains, unwavering. "Poor thing."

He gestures towards the castle while speaking with a baby-like voice and a pinched mouth. "This is your house now. Until I'm bored of you." He purrs.

Chapter 7

I stand there, watching her, the chaos in her eyes a silent pleasure for myself. Aurora, lost in another world, in thoughts, doesn't quite get the gravity of it all.

And I find it amusing, in my own way, because she's a sight to behold when she's panicking. That's already a problem.

Blond golden hair like a cascade of sunlight, framed her face. Those blue eyes, wide and filled with confusion, they're demanding my attention, and I will gladly give them everything they want.

She's short, and I have to admit, it adds a certain charm. She fidgets with the tips of her fingers, her cheeks turning a subtle shade of pink.

It's intriguing, the way she wears her human vulnerability like a delicate cloak. I might be a rude and raw kind of guy, but there's a soft spot for this chaotic beauty. "Well, well, aren't you a vision of perplexity," I chuckle, my voice carrying the rough edge that defines me. "Lost in the in-between, my dear?"

Her gaze darts around, and I can practically see the gears turning in her mind. She's trying to make sense of it all, and it's entertaining to watch.

I lean against the nearest solid thing, which is my castle, crossing my arms, waiting for the realization to hit her like a ton of bricks. "You're not in Vermont anymore," I add, my tone dripping with sarcasm. "Welcome to the nightmare realm. Where, you and me, are the only people breathing." She blinks, seemingly at a loss for words.

I can't help but enjoy the way her confusion paints her face. "Speechless, huh? You look better with words. Maybe you'll figure it out eventually," I tease, a smirk playing on my lips.

She's a puzzle, and I'm looking forward to seeing how to fits all her little pieces.

"Alright, enough with the panic now," I mutter, rolling my eyes at Aurora's bewildered expression.

With a swift and practiced motion, I extend my hand in her direction. The energy in the air shifts, and she looks at me with wide, panicking deer eyes. "Relax, Aurora," I say, my tone softer than usual. "This will make things a bit easier for both of us, but I'm sorry."

I weave the spell with a flick of my wrist, and a soothing glow envelops her. "How do…do you know…my…my nam…" She doesn't have the time to finish a word before, slowly, her eyes flutter closed, and the tension in her shoulders eases.

I catch her just in time, preventing her from collapsing to the ground. She's a fragile doll. "Sleep my dear," I murmur, supporting her weight. "You'll wake up with a clearer head, and maybe, just maybe, less of that panicked charm."

She rests in my arms, the distress that was shining in her eyes is now replaced by a peaceful serenity.

I can't help but acknowledge the strange tenderness that creeps in, hidden beneath the layers.

I turn around, and the castle's imposing door swings open to my sole presence and will.

Stepping into the exterior court, I find myself surrounded by towering walls, with the open sky above. Nightmarish creatures, twisted versions of bats, hover in the clouds, casting eerie shadows.

"Looks like I've got new friends." I realize when seeing the number of crows flying.

Looking down at her, her blond locks spill over my arm like silk, carrying the faint scent of white flowers. The animals above seem to acknowledge my presence, parting to create a path through the sky.

I walk forward, each step resonating against the cold stone beneath us.

The air is heavy with the scent of nightmares, a mix of fear and desperation clinging to the castle walls. Immune to it after all these centuries, I wonder if she can smell it.

Carrying her deeper into the courtyard, my thoughts wander into a self-reflective journey.

Why did I intervene?

In an eternity spent crafting nightmares and molding fears, I've never felt obligated to help any human. Yet, here I am, holding her in my arms, smelling her hair. Aurora, the object of my obsession for the past year.

I've watched her from the shadows, observing the way her fear danced with her strength. Her nightmares intrigued me at first, oceans and screams, but tonight was different.

She was drowning in the depths of this ocean, and for reasons *unknown*, I couldn't stand idly by.

I reached into the turbulent waters of her nightmares and pulled her back to the surface. Unfortunately for me, I brought her into my realm during my panic, and *now* I don't want to let her go anywhere.

The courtyard seems to stretch on endlessly, the flying creatures continue to watch, and their eerie presence adds to the surreal atmosphere. "Shut up," I yell at them while rolling my eyes.

The moment I step into the castle, I take a big breath. *Home*.

The interior is a manifestation of my essence, a sad reflection of my being. Black dominates the space, walls adorned with deep, obsidian hues that seem to absorb any trace of life.

The air is heavy with a scent that reeks of nightmares and regret. *Fucking hell.*

I side-eye the place, for the first time realizing how much it needs some happiness. *Perhaps.*

I drop my eyes on her sleeping mouth, pondering how her voice seems to have awakened something in me. *She's the one who will bring that change in here.*

The decor is a chaotic mix of red accents, splashes of crimson breaking the monotony of darkness. Maximalism prevails, with every corner crammed with oddities and macabre decorations. Skulls adorn the walls alongside abstract paintings that seem to whisper horrors beyond.

Reaching the second room, I approach the bed, the sheets are as black as the rest of the decoration.

I carefully lower Aurora onto the bed, and her soft and pliable body gently sinks into the mattress.

The room have crimson drapes, candles, red roses, and a bath on foot. She'll be ok in here, she'll be safe, clean, fed, and *mine*.

I'll keep her.

Chapter 8

Aurora

I stir from slumber, my eyes fluttering open. The room around me unfolds like a dream or a damn nightmare. I'm expecting to find my colorful walls, my pink and yellow accessories, and all my stuff, but the bed beneath me is a paradise of softness, covered with a luxurious red silk bedsheet that seems straight out of royalty.

Obviously not mine.

The room is vast, embracing me in its dimensions. The walls are painted in a deep black, creating an elegant contrast against the large wood furniture that stands with an imposing grace.

I lean on my forearms, focusing my eyes on the rest of the room, the windows, *oh*, they're something out of a fairytale. Large and curvy, they're framed in ornate wood, like a portal to another world.

I can't quite see outside sitting on the bed, but I glance toward them, and a pang of realization strikes. There's no sunlight streaming through, no warm rays casting a golden glow.

It's disconcerting, there's no bright light that I usually wake up to.

Wake up, just wake up.

I sit up fully, the silk cover sliding gracefully off me. I swing my legs over the side of the bed, the plush carpet beneath feels like a cloud under my feet.

The absence of sunlight, the grandeur of the windows, the black and red aesthetics—it's all so confusing. This can't be real.

THE MAN!

There was a man, beautiful, tall, and with what seemed to be pointy ears, in front of me.

We were outside.

Why am I here? Where is he?

I let out a gentle sigh, feeling curious with lots of questions popping up in my mind.

My bare feet touch the soft carpet as I move toward the large windows, drawn by an inexplicable pull to see what lies beyond.

I walk closer and gasp, my hands flying to cover my mouth as I take in the sight before me.

The outside world unfolds like a painting. The sky is an unusual shade of green, unlike anything I've ever seen. It stretches on endlessly, giving the surroundings an eerie and surreal feeling.

Like earlier.

Bats and birds swirl around in a chaotic dance, their shapes casting shadows on what appears to be a courtyard in the center of the castle.

It's both creepy and beautiful at the same time.

I look further and notice a dark stretch of woods on the horizon, the same ones I passed through. The trees loom tall and intimidating, blending almost seamlessly with the shadows.

Despite their menacing appearance, there's a strange beauty in the darkness.

I attempt to understand my surroundings, to comprehend the reality of where I am. The man's words linger in my mind, urging me to make sense of it all. "Welcome to the nightmare realms. Where, you and me, are the only people breathing."

I feel the impact of his words sinking in, and I'm left wrestling with the surreal reality of it all.

Nightmare realms?

The more I try to make sense of things, the more my head starts to throb. It's like a storm in there, and I'm caught in the middle. Desperation starts to sink in.

I turn around, hoping for something, anything, to distract me. There's a big, comfy-looking chair, and next to it, a stunning black porcelain bath that catches my eye. It's a beauty, but my attention shifts to the chair again.

Is this…a dress?

Yes. There's a dress, hanging there as if waiting for me.

Simple and airy, it's made of a fabric I've never seen before.

It's like fog and something solid at the same time, with delicate little straps. The dress has a white base with a hint of blue-grey, a color that feels oddly soothing.

Curiosity getting the better of me, I pick up the dress. It's as soft as a dream, and as I examine its details, a paper falls to the floor.

Hello, my dear.
Sorry for the forced sleep, you were insupportable.
This dress is for you.
Take a bath if you wish.

Chapter 9

Aurora

Wow! I can't believe this is happening to me right now. I'm twirling around in this enchanting dress, and it feels like a dream – *but…it is.*

I've never seen a dress quite like this one before. The fabric, *oh*, the fabric! It's like a gentle whisper against my skin as if it's made of stardust and wishes.

I glance down at the dress, its ethereal folds cascading around me in a dance of colors that seem to shimmer and change with every movement.

This bath also helped. I was nasty, dirty from the forest floor dirt, and sweat.

It's a shame I didn't have any makeup, but I feel pretty good, especially since none of it is real.

A little giggle escapes me, and I can't help but twirl again, the dress floating around me. I feel like a character from a whimsical fairy tale, the protagonist in her magical attire, living in a world painted with imagination.

There's still no sunlight here, and it's been two hours since I woke up.

How can there be no sun?

I'm looking at one of the big windows baffles when my tummy's doing its own thinking. *Loudly.*

"Shit, I'm hungry," I speak to myself.

Deciding it's time to leave this room, I swing open the door. The air feels different – chillier.

I step out into the castle, and I'm surprised by its size. It's kind of small but super weird.

Everything's dark – and lots of dead animal stuff. And the paintings?

Totally creepy.

But I don't feel scared like I did in that spooky forest. I continue walking, looking in each crooked door, searching for food and the man who brought me here and left that note.

Maybe he'll know why there's no sun and why the heck I'm here. I know we spoke, but the sleep I fell into hit me like a heavy weight and my mind seems hazy since I woke up.

As I wander through the castle halls, I don't encounter anyone. It's like a ghost town, devoid of life or sound. No souls at all, not even a maid.

The castle's corridors lead me to a grand room. A massive chandelier hangs from the ceiling, twinkling with candlelight.

With every step closer, the sensation of someone's presence intensifies. It's like a gentle pull, urging me toward the heart of this mysterious room.

I reach the entrance; my eyes widen at the sight.

In the soft illumination of the candles, there he is – the man. His short white hair, like a silvery crown, and a lone lock falls on his forehead. He's sitting at a massive table, all alone, engrossed in what seems to be parchment filled with mysterious writings.

The room itself feels ancient like it's holding secrets from a time long ago.

The man is dressed all in black, and as my eyes adjust, I notice something– his ears are pointy. Like, really pointy.

I knew it. Did I for real dream of an elf?

My eyes widen with surprise, and a soft gasp escapes my lips. This is no ordinary man. He's a monster, giant on his chair, looking like he's seven foot tall.

I take a moment to observe him. His gaze is focused, and there's an air of wisdom around him. The flickering light casts a soft glow on his features, giving him an almost ethereal look.

Summoning my courage, I clear my throat and speak, my voice echoing in the vast room. "Um, hi there! I was, uh, wandering around. Thanks for the dress. I'm Aurora."

The man looks up, his gaze meeting mine, and for a moment, the room feels still. There's a depth in his pale blue eyes.

A small smile plays on his lips and dimples form at their corners as he acknowledges my presence. "Aurora," he says in a voice that resonates like a distant melody. "I already know you."

My heart races with a mix of excitement and curiosity.

Slow down, heart.

"Aurora," He repeats for himself, closing his eyes, his voice a low rumble. I feel the heat flushing my pale cheeks.

He gestures for me to take a seat, and I do so, my airy dress making a soft swish as I settle into a chair. "You're the one who stumbled into my domain." The smile is gone, replaced by a menacing look.

I can't help but smile, undeterred by his rough exterior. "Well, you see, I was in a nightmare. And BOOM. Then I was in the forest. Woke up in this dreamy castle, and I got this magical dress. It's amazing, by the way! And I thought, 'Why not explore?'" I gesture around the room with wide-eyed enthusiasm.

He arches an eyebrow, "Magical dress, you say? Exploring, huh?" He leans back, folding his arms across his chest. "Quite the adventurer, aren't you, Aurora? Not everyone stumbles into the nightmare realm and lives to tell the tale."

I giggle, the bubbly sound filling the silence. "Well, I'm not like everyone else, I guess. I mean, it's my dream after all. And you, Mr., you're like the mysterious character who holds all the secrets. What's your name?"

He snorts a rough sound that reverberates through the castle walls. "Secrets, huh? Do you think you can handle them, little adventurer? Not everyone appreciates the truth I'm Nyx."

Nyx. Nyx. Nyx. Nyx. Nyx.

Such a beautiful name.

I tilt my head, my optimism undiminished. "I love stories, even the raw and gritty ones. They make life interesting! So, why am I here? In the nightmare realm? What's the story behind this magical castle, and why did you give me this incredible dress?"

Nyx chuckles, that's more cynical than amused. "You're full of questions, my dear. But if you must know, this castle is simply my house. As for the dress, it's a gift – a reminder that not everything is what it seems."

I nod, absorbing his words. "So, what are you if you are living here? And can I wake up now?"

Nyx leans forward, his pale blue eyes meeting mine. "Don't get too comfortable, Aurora. Not all tales have happy endings. You speak to me like I'm your friend. I'm a God, and you should address me like so."

I smile, unfazed by his ominous words. "Well, Mr. God Nyx, I'm happy to have met you. But I can go home now."

He chuckles again, a bit softer this time. "You are a weird human. Don't you realize what's going on? You are awake. I took you and brought you into my realm."

Chapter 10

Aurora

I stare at him, a perplexed expression etched across my face. "Um, what the... what does that even mean?" I mumble, trying to wrap my head around Nyx's enigmatic statement.

He leans back, his eyes narrowing as he watches my reaction. "It means, that this realm is not all rainbows and sunshine, and I'm the God of it. It means I kidnap you. It means I want to keep you here, for a time."

I blink, still processing his words when he suddenly stands up, breaking the intensity of the moment. "Enough talk for now. You must be hungry."

Nyx opens a cabinet, grabs some food, and places it on the table in front of me.

But instead of focusing on the food, I'm lost in a whirlwind of confusion and discomfort. It's like the air around me is getting thicker, making it hard to breathe. I'm staring at his face, my mind a chaotic mess of thoughts.

Nyx glances at me, a hint of impatience in his eyes. "Eat," he grumbles, his tone less harsh than before.

"I can't... I can't," I stammer, feeling a tightness in my chest. "It's like... everything is spinning, and I can't catch my breath."

Nyx sighs, irritation, and concern on his face. "Great, just great. You're not going to pass out on me, are you?" He pulls up a chair, sitting across from me and waving a hand in front of my face. "Focus, Aurora. Breathe. In and out."

"I'm trying," I gasp, struggling to follow his instructions.

The space seems to be shrinking around me, and my mind is a jumble of confusion.

Nyx rolls his eyes, his expression softening slightly. "Look, it's not that complicated. In... and out. Slowly." He mimics deep breaths, and I try to follow his lead, attempting to regain control over my racing heart.

After a few moments, the tightness in my chest eases, and the dizziness begins to subside.

I blink, realizing that Nyx's rather unorthodox and rude method actually helped. "Thanks," I manage to say, my voice shaky but grateful.

Nyx grumbles something unintelligible, but there's a hint of relief in his eyes. "Just eat. We've got a lot to talk about, and you won't get far on an empty stomach."

I tentatively take a bite of the food. Nyx may be rough around the edges, *kidnapped me like he said*, but it seems there's more to him than meets the eye.

I'm sitting at this massive dining table, munching on bread, cheeses, and grapes. The food is good, and my body feels happy and full.

The castle's quiet now, just the sound of me chewing and the distant creaks of this old place and probably these weird ass bats outside.

Nyx, the God.

The perfect, chiseled jaw, muscular god.

Left me alone after my almost panic attack. Without a word, just massaging the nape of his neck looking on the verge of breaking my mine with irritation and walked away.

I should be panicking, right? I mean, I'm in a mysterious castle with a grumpy god named Nyx who talks in riddles and literally menacing to keep me.

But here's the thing – I choose not to panic.

Why Aurora?

Because Nyx might be the only key to getting out of this mess. And if I want to make it, I've got to play it cool.

I look around the room, and the thought of Nyx somewhere in the estate makes me a little nervous. I take a deep breath, trying to steady my nerves, and continue nibbling on a grape.

My heart skips a beat as Nyx's voice suddenly appears beside me. "Aurora, my dear, come with me for a walk." I jump in surprise, nearly knocking over my chair. "FUCK!" I yell, trying to calm my poor heart.

Nyx smirks, a glint of amusement in his pale blue eyes. "So jumpy. Just follow me." He turns on his heel and strides away, leaving me with no choice but to scamper after him.

We stroll side by side, and I'm forced to notice the intense height difference between us. I'm five foot four, and he's easily towering above me. It's like walking alongside a moody giant.

"So, Nyx," I begin, my curiosity taking control. "How did you end up being a God? It sounds kind of cool, but also, um, unreal. And why keeping me?"

Nyx glances down at me, his hands nonchalantly tucked into the pockets of his black pants. "A lot of questions for this pretty mouth of yours."

I pout playfully. "Aw, come on! I want to know, especially the part about me being here!"

He chuckles, a deep sound that wakes up a part of me I had forgotten. "You're persistent, I'll give you that. Fine, I am born a God. My mother was one of the goddesses working in the paradise realm. My father was the previous God of the nightmare realm. It's a duty, not a choice."

I tilt my head, absorbing his words. "Duty, huh? Sounds like a big responsibility. But... wait a minute. Did you just say that there's another realm?" I ask, astonished.

Nyx's gaze shifts ahead, his expression unreadable. "There's multiples. Each one is on a different island. There's paradise, redemption, war, nature, death, dreams, and" He stops and gestures around him, the green atmosphere circling us now that we are on the exterior. "Nightmare. This world is called the Godsland."

Chapter 11

Aurora

)———∘◇∘———(

OK. That's an awful lot of information to comprehend.

We walk slowly, and I note tall and beautiful bushes, their leaves, a deep, velvety green,

They remind me of the forest behind my house. My little house, I sigh and focus my gaze on the ground. "Are you sad?" Nyx asks, his tone nonchalant.

I roll my eyes and stop moving. "Seriously? You kidnap me, tell me you have no intention of letting me go, claim you're a god, and you think it wouldn't bother me? Yes, I'm sad and angry." Time seems to stand still, and the only sound is the wind weaving through the flowers, their colors a captivating blend of red, white, and black. "And would you be less angry if I told you that, I saw you drowning in your nightmare? So, I pulled you out of there and saved your life?" Nyx smirks, pride in his eyes.

And he resumes walking as if nothing happened. "Maybe." I grimace and cross my arms over my chest, trailing behind him.

I twirl a lock of my hair between my fingers, pondering his words. "But that doesn't explain why you felt the need to save me from my nightmare or keep me here. I don't know you. And to be honest, I'm not even sure if all this conversation isn't some kind of dream I'm having."

Nyx stops walking, turning to face me with his eyebrows furrowed slightly. "You were dying, Aurora. When people have a nightmare, if they die in it, they die in real life too. And trust me, you are not in a dream. I can't control or create dreams. That's Morphea's deal." He growls, visibly annoyed with all my blabbering.

I blink, absorbing his words. *So, not a dream. Fuck.*

"Got it, Mr. God Nyx. Anything else I should know?"

The echo of his footsteps filling the air is his only response for a while.

"Just remember, my dear, this realm is full of surprises, and not all of them are pleasant. Be cautious, be aware, and stop fucking annoying me."

"I just want to understand what's going on. I have the right. I have friends and a job. I can't just disappear like that." I start to get angry, heat rising to my cheeks.

He stops and turns to face me in one swift motion, his powerful hand finding my chin and gripping it firmly, using the tip of his index finger to stroke my lower lip.

A low growl escapes his throat just as he rolls his head and closes his eyes.

"Let me make this clear, I save you, you owe me. I'll answer all your silly questions, because yes, you have the right. But your," he tightens his grip a bit more, "friends, I've seen them. Your bakery and your little ridiculous apron full of colors, I've seen those too."

My traitorous body seems to want to give in. My knees are weak, and I find no strength to push him away. The warmth of his finger sliding over my mouth, his face so close to mine.

His breath on my face and the way his eyes burn onto mine. *It's been so long I didn't feel wanted like this.*

"Fuck, Gods, Aurora. I want to keep you in locks forever." He purrs. His mouth is dangerously close to mine.

My gaze doesn't leave his. "You seem to have a cold heart, Mr. God."

He brings his slightly open mouth even closer to mine; I close my eyes and let an involuntary moan-sigh escape my lips.

"This is what happens when you are alone for centuries."

"Does it feel lonely?" I ask, breathless, on the verge of breaking.

His dark eyebrows seem to lift a bit higher, and I focus on his eyes. What I see in them could almost break my heart.

Sadness, I'm sure it's sadness. I recognize that.

"Gods never feel loneliness."

He licks his lips, and I part mine.

Before I have time to do anything, to understand what's happening, or even to reason with myself to step back, he releases my face abruptly and runs a hand through his white hair.

"Gods are not allowed to leave their islands. Each must remain on theirs forever. Exceptionally, twice a year, the gods who oversee the paradise island organize parties where Vion, the king of the gods, allows everyone to go."

His gaze becomes evasive, and he no longer looks me in the eyes. Meanwhile, I try to calm the uncontrollable beats of my heart.

"We can travel into the world of humans. See, and hear, but impossible to interact with you or even just talk. But believe me, Aurora." His blue orbs, also with silver reflections, plunge back into mine. "I have watched you."

Is it normal if I'm super turned on right now?

"Oh. I see. That's weird." Is the only thing I answer, and I want to punch myself.

"I should go. I have other nightmares to send to the pathetic mortals of your world. You can walk wherever you want. All the places on my island are open to you."

I'm left standing alone in the haunting stillness of the castle courtyard. The fucker just disappeared in a cloud of black and grey fog.

With a deep breath, I decide to retreat into the castle, leaving the cool night air behind.

The grand corridors welcome me back.

I roam aimlessly, guided by the dim glow of flickering candles.

That's so weird because there's clearly electricity in here, I've seen a numeric clock in one of the rooms on a little table, and the bathtub had a regular drain and all, but he still uses candles to light up the place.

I'll need to ask about that.

I wander deeper into this silent home; my steps lead me to an ornate door.

Pushing it open reveals a vast library. The shelves are lined with ancient books, their leather spines worn with time. The scent of old paper fills the air, creating an atmosphere of both comfort and wonder. "Wow," I murmur.

I find myself drawn to the shelves, running my fingers along the edges of the books.

He said everything was open to me. So, I must have the right to read his books.

I select one with a brown cover and beautiful flowers painted on top of it, and settle into a big reading chair, eager to immerse myself in the stories and secrets that await within the pages.

Chapter 12

)———⬦———(

Sitting on this plush red chair in Nyx's extraordinary library adds to this weird new reality of mine, one that I'm still not entirely sure is real. The air is filled with the comforting fragrance of musty scents with a touch of wood and ink, and I can't help but let out a little squeal of joy.

I've got this massive book on my lap, and *oh boy*, it's practically begging me to dive into its magical pages. Gently, I brush away the dust that's settled on the cover.

Opening it with care, I'm greeted by the mesmerizing world of plants and nature in the

Godsland. The vibrant illustrations dance off the pages, and I feel the excitement building inside me.

Immediately, my gaze is drawn to the section on black lotus trees. It's like the book is shouting at me to pay attention to this stunning illustration.

I read the text beside the picture, learning that these trees exist in both the human realm and the Godsland realm.

But here's the interesting part – in the Godsland realm, their existence was banished long ago by the king of gods, Vion.

According to legends, these trees, with their long, sharp thorns, used to amplify the powers of the gods and even grant new ones. I gasp and eagerly turn the page.

If the gods were daring enough to pierce their divine flesh where their hearts were with those thorns, they'd get an instant power boost.

I take a breath, stop reading, and look at the wall, thinking about all of this.

The king of gods wasn't too thrilled about this whole situation, *clearly*. He was probably worried that things were getting a bit too wild up in the Godsland realm, and starting to make decisions on their own.

So, he waved his mighty divine hand and banished the black lotus trees from the realm. No more power-boosting acupuncture for the gods, so all the power to him.

Suddenly, I remember Nyx mentioning the upcoming festivities, and my curiosity got the better of me. I dove into this massive book to find some juicy details. But navigating through this brick of information is like wandering through a magical maze!

Legends, prophecies, medical treatments, power lineages – it's a whirlwind of words that's making my head spin.

I flip through the pages, my eyes darting from one intricate illustration to another, trying to find a hint about the festivities. But the more I read, the more it feels like I'm tumbling down a rabbit hole of ancient knowledge.

I flip through the massive book, searching for information, and my eyes catch on something unexpected. It's a section about creatures from the Godsland, and there, right in front of me, is a breathtaking illustration of a dragon with the inscription, Umbrosus.

I can't help but stare in awe at the majestic creature, its scales shimmering in the light. For a moment, I forget all about what I was looking for and lose myself in the wonder of the drawing.

My finger glides slowly over the illustration, I read the text beside it. It tells the story of the last dragon, a magnificent creature that met its end at the hands of Vion when he destroyed the god of the death realm.

It's a tragic tale, and I can't help but feel a pang of sadness for the loss of such a magnificent being.

According to the book, the dragon was one of the last remaining creatures of the original Gods. Now they can be created in nightmares and dreams but they are imitations, not real, not flesh and blood. Only imagination and shadows.

They were the companions of the death god. Helping to travel and help in wars in the human realm.

Intrigued by the mention of Vion and the gods, I grab another book from the shelf. Its title, "Histories," promises to shed light on the ancient tales of the deities.

With eager anticipation, I quickly flip through the pages, scanning the text for any mention of Vion and his role.

As I read, I learn that in the beginning, there existed a single god who presided over both death and war.

However, as this god sought to expand his influence and power, Vion was forced to intervene. In an act of divine judgment, Vion killed this god and split the realm into two separate islands.

Now, Vion rules over the realm of death, while another god oversees the realm of war.

It's a fascinating revelation, shedding new light on the intricate dynamics of the divine hierarchy.

I turn the page quickly.

The first gods are named the other originals. And besides the death and war ones, all the others had already departed for the Universe of Repose, a retirement realm for gods.

I sit there, lost in thought, pondering the significance of what I've just read.

Feeling a bit overwhelmed, I decide to close the book. Closing my eyes, I lean back into the plushness of the chair, letting my head rest against its support.

In the darkness behind my closed eyelids, I can almost see the swirl of legends and prophecies dancing like elusive shadows.

It's like trying to catch fireflies – beautiful, but fleeting.

The weight in my head gradually starts to lift, replaced by a sense of calm.

Maybe I need a moment to let all this information settle. I'll come back to the book later, with fresh eyes and a clearer mind.

For now, a nap in the quiet embrace of Nyx's library is just what I need.

Chapter 13

Aurora

I awaken to the sensation of something soft slipping off my shoulder. Blinking groggily, I look down to see a cozy fur blanket draped over me. Confusion clouds my thoughts – I certainly didn't have a blanket when I drifted off.

And where are all the books? The library appears unnervingly tidy.

Pushing aside the blanket, I sit up and stretch, the fabric crumpling at my feet. It's an odd sensation, but I feel surprisingly warm and refreshed.

For the first time in what feels like ages, I've slept without the relentless grip of nightmares weighing me down.

No more cries echoing in my ears, no more eerie sounds of bubbling water.

It's as though I've been enveloped in a cocoon of sweet darkness and tranquility. The absence of bad dreams feels like a gift I never knew I needed.

And right now, I'm feeling downright fantastic.

With newfound energy coursing through my veins, I leap out of the chair and begin stretching in exaggerated positions, humming little tunes to myself.

I'm on a high from this newfound sense of peace.

During one particularly amusing stretch, I bend forward, placing my face between my legs, only to find Nyx leaning casually against the doorframe, wearing a sly grin.

Shirtless.

His arms are crossed over his bare chest, and his damp hair falling on his forehead.

I can't tear my gaze away from him for even a second. His toned stomach and the tantalizing V-shaped muscles draw my attention like a magnet.

And those pants... well, let's just say they leave little to the imagination. "Love what are you looking at, darling?"

I freeze, my head upside down between my legs, caught off guard. Nyx is just standing there, all nonchalant, with that mischievous glint in his eyes.

My cheeks heat up, and I can't help but stammer a surprised "Hello."

It's a little awkward, but he seems to be enjoying the fact that my face is probably red as a tomato.

The air in the room feels charged with a different kind of energy. I straighten up, smiling at him with all my teeth.

Nyx, with that predatory gaze, starts walking towards me, and the air stocks in my throat.

"Hey, Nyx," I manage to say, my voice a bit breathless. "Why didn't I have nightmares? It's like the best sleep I've had in forever." I try to change my mind, and start a conversation that maybe will make him stop walking towards me.

I'm supposed to hate him for fuck sakes.

He smirks, circling me slowly, and I catch a hint of silver shining in his eyes. "In the GodsLand, no one can dream. It's a luxury only the mortal realm gets to enjoy."

His presence distracts me. He's close now, and I feel his hot breath on my skin. It sends shivers down my spine.

"Enjoying the peace, are you?" he whispers in one of my ears, his voice low.

I nod, trying to focus on the conversation. "Yeah, it's just... different."

Nyx continues to circle me, like a predator assessing its prey. His gaze intensifies, and he leans in, sniffing the air around me.

The tension in the room is palpable. *

"Why are you so different, Aurora?" he murmurs, his breath grazing my ear.

I struggle to find words, the heat building inside me. "I... I don't know."

He chuckles a gravely, throaty sound. "I can sense it, you know."

His words hang in the air as he continues to circle, the tension escalating with every step. My heart is pounding so hard I'm sure he can hear it, "Why would you say humans are lucky to dream?" I ask.

"Because, when I started to be obsessed with you. I wanted to feel you, to touch you, to *fuck* you. Since I was not authorized to do it for real. I wished day and night that I could dream of you."

OK. I...Fuck.

Nyx's hands trace along my skin, and a shiver dances down my spine. I stammer, "Wait if you're the god of nightmares, does that mean you've been the one giving me those awful dreams all this time?"

A sly smile plays on his lips as he nods. "Guilty as charged, my dear Aurora. But I had my reasons."

Anger climbs fucking fast up within me, mixing with heat already there on my face.

I'm burning.

I blurt out, "Well, I don't appreciate it. And so, I don't appreciate you."

He continues to circle, his touch leaving a trail of fire on my skin. "Anger suits you, my dear. Would you like to show me how much you hate me?"

I take a deep breath, trying to compose myself. "But why? Why give nightmares?"

Nyx stops circling and looks me square in the eyes. "The fear, the anxiety, the thrill – it's a necessity for you to affront them, to move on."

I narrow my eyes, frustration taking over. "I don't want to move on if it implies revisiting my trauma. I want peaceful nights. I deserve that much."

He leans in, his lips almost brushing against mine and I close my eyes. "Deserve? Mortals rarely get what they deserve, but sometimes, they get what they need."

I look into his cold eyes, a defiant fire burning in mine. "Well, I don't need your nightmares. I'm tired of being haunted."

Nyx's gaze softens for a moment, and then he chuckles. "Fuck. The effect you have on me."

Chapter 14

Aurora's skin is like silk under my fingertips. Soft, so *fucking* soft.

The dress I made for her feels unnecessary right now. I look at her, rough hands tracing her curves. She shivers as I touch her, and I'm so hard.

"Don't need this dress, do you?" I croon, fingers gliding up her arms. I take the strap between two calloused fingers and start lowering it, slowly.

Her breath catches, and she meets my eyes, a fire burning between us. "Tell me you want it off," I demand, my voice low and rough. Aurora bites her lip, eyes locked with mine, desire dancing in her blue iris.

The need to taste her builds up to a painful high as the strap slips down, revealing more of her skin. I growl and lean my body forward to eliminate the few inches that separate us.

My hands find her waist, fingers gripping firmly. Pressing my form against hers, I grind my erection on her waist, letting her know the power she has over me.

"Tell me, Aurora," I growl, lips brushing against her ear, "tell me you want this damn dress off." My voice is a low rumble, and I feel the goosebumps on her skin beneath my touch.

I trail kisses down her neck, tracing the curve of her shoulder. Her breath hitches, and she finally whispers, "I want it off, Nyx."

A smirk plays on my lips as I continue my assault on her neck, hands moving with purpose. The dress becomes an obstacle, and I make quick work of the remaining straps, letting it fall to the floor.

Skin on skin, desire burning like wildfire, I'm almost completely out of control.

One fucking year.

One year of obsession with her. Watching her, day and night.

Crafting her nightmare with little information her mind gave me, I wish I could have taken something less traumatic, but for some reason, there was nothing else to use.

I was hoping to help her surpass her fear and her trauma. Make her stronger.

But my darling was drowning, and I couldn't let that happen.

Screw the rules, screw the *King*.

One year, of jerking myself off alone in this cursed realm thinking about the taste of her skin.

My hands explore, rough and possessive, as I revel in the softness of her skin. Aurora's fingers grip my shoulders, nails digging in, urging me closer.

I lift her, instinct taking over, and her legs wrap around my waist. There's a frantic wildness in our movements, desire, and need.

Her naked body against mine, the only remaining clothes is my pants. I clench my teeth together when the wetness of her cunt passes through my pants

Our mouths collide in a heated exchange, tongues wrestling for dominance. I guide her towards the edge of a table, the cold surface probably biting her ass cheeks.

"Tell me, my dear" I command, a low breath escaping my lips, "tell me how much you want this."

Her response is a breathless affirmation, a primal plea that only fuels the fire boiling in me.

I take a step back, my gaze fixated on her, naked and spread on the table just for me.

Perfection.

The flickering candlelight casts shadows, highlighting every curve of her body, her pink nipple pointing at me.

I grab my erection hard through my pants and bite the inside of my cheek as I appreciate the sight before me, satisfaction evident in my eyes. "You're a damn masterpiece, Aurora," I raspy, my voice thick with lust.

"Can you stop looking at me like that?" She asks, almost Inaudibly.

Reaching out, I run my hands along her thighs, fingers tracing patterns that leave goosebumps in their wake.

Forcing her legs to stay open before me, I drop my gaze on her glistening pussy. "Never. I'll never stop looking at you. At your perfection. And if one day I stop, please kill me." I respond.

I feel her tremble under my touch, and she moans softly at my words. "I shouldn't." She breathes for herself.

With a sudden motion, I pull her to the edge of the table, her eyes locking onto mine.

Kneeling in front of her, I take her foot in my hands, my lips grazing the delicate skin.

My tongue traces slow, tantalizing circles, and I feel her muscles loosen under my touch in response.

Slowly, I trail my way up her leg, leaving a fiery path of my mark. I sink my teeth into the flesh, a controlled bite that elicits a gasp of pleasure and pain from her.

Her reaction fuels me, and I can't help but smile at the sound.

I pull back and glance at the teeth marks on her skin. With a wicked grin, I lick the area, savoring the salty taste of her, licking her wounds.

"Mine," I murmur, the word a possessive growl that hangs in the air.

Chapter 15

Aurora

I can't think clearly anymore. All my decisions, all my intentions, have flown away with him licking and grazing his teeth on my inner thigh. The heat between us is unbearable, and I feel my pussy dripping with anticipation. I look down and the sight and almost orgasm on the spot. He's looking right as his finger sliding up and down my opening, spreading my juices all over my lips, mouth open, tongue licking his lips.

An inaudible gasp escapes me as he pushes his finger inside me.

The same inch. *In. Out. In. Out.*

I'm in disbelief at the scene before me when his eyes find mine. "You love it, don't you?"

But I can't respond, I'm too speechless.

He lowers his mouth close to my skin and bites down on the side of my pussy, hard.

"Ouch!" I breathe, my eyes watering.

"Tell me, darling, how bad do you want this?" He asks while pushing his fingers completely inside my core.

I gasp, the sensation sending a jolt of insupportable heat in me.

"You're soaking wet for me," He purred, a proud grin spreading across his too-beautiful face. "No need for words, your body's doing all the talking. Listen this cunt sing for me"

I give up.

Shamelessly start grinding up and down my body on his fingers, closing my eyes and letting go of all I thought was right, chasing the climax I crave right now. The wet sound of my arousal splashing against his strong hand pushes me deeper into the madness.

He lowers his mouth, hot breath sending tremors through me. his lips find their mark, and he feasts on me like a maniac.

Finger fucking me at the same time, rough, primal, and so goddam good. A loud moan escapes me as I feel the ecstasy coming.

"You feel so good," He murmurs between licks, his lips moving on my clitoris.

As the intensity builds, I glance down, locking eyes with him. "Are you mine?" He growls, a satisfied grin spreading across his face.

The room echoes with the symphony of our shared sigh of pleasure. "Y…Yes." I answer.

He intensifies the movements, attuned to the moans and breaths of my pleasure.

My legs start trembling and the inside of my belly begins to spasm. I arch my back, a breathless cry escaping my lips. My body explodes with my climax, and I maintain the connection, savoring the intimacy of the moment still grinding the last waves of my orgasm "Yes you are," He murmurs, his voice possessive.

I stand up from the table, starting to feel shy without my clothes now that the high has ended. I try to cover myself, but Nyx looks at me with a kind of annoyance.

I know I'm ridiculous, the man just put his mouth on my pussy.

"Hey," he says, his hand gently grazing my cheek. "Don't hide." His voice is still husky.

With a wave of his hand, a dress appears around me. The gown is super pretty, mixing red and black. The material feels smooth and looks fancy as it flows down. The top part is like a corset, making my curves look nice.

There's this cool lace stuff all around, making beautiful designs. The dress shape is amazing, fitting nicely and then flowing down to the ground.

"There," he smiles.

"But I don't have underwear," I laugh.

"I know." He keeps looking at me like he's admiring a piece of art.

I offer Nyx a sincere "Thank you," He responds with a soft smile.

Fuck me, those dimples.

Capturing my lips in a gentle kiss, he whispers against my mouth. "You're welcome,"

As we pull away, our eyes lock. "This time, I took it easy, I was gentle, but next time won't be as soft," he affirms with a tone shift, a warning and a promise wrapped into one

I nod, "Do you do this often?" I dare.

Am I jealous?

Nyx's gaze doesn't waver as he responds, "I've known many humans, Aurora. I don't even know how many centuries I've been alive."

I press further, needing to understand. "What happens after?" I inquire, my voice steady but with a hint of vulnerability.

He considers my question, a thoughtful pause hanging in the air before he speaks. "Usually, I returned them to their world, but what we have, it's more than that. No one had been like you."

"And if I don't want it?" I ask, a bit frustrated to know there were others before me.

You should be mad he wants to keep you, dumbass.

Nyx's expression shifts. "Unfortunately for you, you're stuck here, my dear" he adds.

My heart sinks the weight of his responses heavy on my shoulders. I had a plan, I had a future, and all of this wasn't part of it.

Nyx looks at me with a hint of mischief in his eyes, his fingers tracing a playful path along my cheek. "Wait for me. I'll go get dressed, clean up a little bit and we will head out after."

As he turns to leave, a surge of curiosity prompts me to ask, "What time is it?" The uncertainty of time in this realm gnaws at me, with this constant green-dark sky I can't tell if it's night or day.

He glances back, a smirk playing on his lips. "There's no time here, but in mortal terms, it's morning."

I remember a numeric clock I've seen in here, and I can't help but question its presence. "Why do you have a clock if there's no time here?" I demand, trying to make sense of the contradiction.

Nyx winks at me, a mischievous glint in his silvery-blue eyes, but before I can think more about things deeply, while he goes away.

"Where are we going?" I call after him, unable to contain my curiosity.

He sighs in frustration and turns to face me. "You're so damn annoying with your questions," he retorts, his tone tinged with exasperation.

I can't help but smile brightly at Nyx's exasperation.

Bouncing over to him, I pose with my hands on his chest, looking up with an impish grin and he almost flinches.

Interesting.

"Well, if I don't ask questions, how will I ever annoy you enough to let me go?" I say in a bubbly tone.

The frustration in Nyx's expression softens, replaced by a reluctant amusement.

He rolls his eyes but can't hide a smirk. "Just be ready."

Chapter 16

Aurora

⟩————◇————⟨

As Nyx and I step out of the castle, my mind is still grappling with the notion that I might be in some bizarre dream.

It's impossible for me to just be in the Godsland like that. It really must be a dream.

But at the same time, I can't ignore anymore that I'm happy here. If my emotions and the way my body reacts to Nyx's touch aren't enough to convince me, the books I've read earlier are real. I'm convinced of it. With their information and their answers to so many questions.

Hands on my belly, I try to control my breathing.

Inhale. Exhale.

Okay.

I look from left to right, listening carefully. Nyx is gone, and I need to catch up with him, but before that, there's still something I want to do.

I peek around the doorframe, checking for Nyx. No sign of him.

Heart pounding, I dart down the hallway, careful not to make a sound. I reach the library and scan the shelves frantically. Potions, powers, humans, animals, and there it is, medicinal & Umbrosus.

Yes, that's the one.

I open the book and flip through the pages until I find the section on the recent history of creatures in the Godsland. If there were original dragons for the god of death and war, there must have been others for the other gods, and I'm really curious about what happened to them.

My face twists in a grimace, lips thinning, as I tear out the pages. I stuff them under my pillow and hurry back to my room.

I don't know if I'll get another chance to visit the library so, I needed to do it now.

I smooth down my dress, making sure it lays just right. Nyx's touch lingers on my skin, sending shivers down my spine. I will never be able to shake the memory of it, nor do I want to.

I walk down the hallway, lost in my thoughts. Each step brings me closer to the front door, closer to seeing Nyx again.

I reach the entryway with its big wooden front door. The place gives me goosebumps. It's dark and so silent, with weird paintings hanging on the walls.

One painting catches my eye. It's like a black hole in the ground, the sky green and creepy, *like outside.*

In the middle, there's a deformed skeleton, looking like it's screaming. Around it, blurry figures are falling into the black hole. They seem scared too.

Looking at the painting gives me a strange feeling, of unease.

I quickly turn away, trying to shake off the creepy feeling that's settled over me.

As I turn, my heart skips a beat. There he is, Nyx, standing tall and breathtakingly beautiful. His serious expression sends a pang of disappointment through me, but I refuse to let it dampen my spirits.

"Hey there, handsome," I chirp, mustering up my brightest smile.

Nyx's gaze meets mine, but instead of melting into a smile, his eyes remain cold and distant. It's like staring into a glacier, all icy and impenetrable. My smile falters, but I press on, determined to lighten the mood.

"I was admiring the artwork?" I gesture towards the painting, trying to inject some levity into the tense atmosphere.

Nyx follows my gesture, his eyes lingering on the disturbing scene depicted on the canvas. "That painting?" he says, his voice low and tinged with bitterness. "It's my father's work."

I'm taken aback by his somber tone, the weight of his words hanging heavy in the air. "Your father?" I echo, unsure of how to respond. "It's kind of beautiful."

And it's the truth. The colors, the brushstrokes, it's truly beautiful. Even though it's very dark.

Nyx nods, his expression unreadable. "He was good."

I study the painting again, seeing it in a new light now that I know its creator. The twisted figures and ominous void take on a deeper significance, reflecting the darkness that must have consumed Nyx's father.

"It's... hauntingly beautiful, for real" I murmur, searching for the right words. "But also... unsettling."

Nyx's gaze softens slightly, a flicker of emotion passing through his eyes. "That's one way to describe it," he says quietly. "But it's also a reminder of the darkness that runs in my blood. I'm, after all, crafting nightmares."

"Enough talk. Anyway, you're supposed to hate me, remember," Nyx says abruptly, his voice cutting through the solemn air. "Let's walk together."

His command takes me by surprise, but I nod.

He's right.

There's a tension between us, a silent understanding that some things are better left unsaid. Without another word, Nyx gestures for me to follow him, and together we step out of the shadowy room and into the humongous door frame.

Chapter 17

Aurora

)———◇◇◇———(

We walk side by side, and it's impossible not to steal glances at Nyx. His features are chiseled and striking. The tiny beard stubble barely two or three days old. But there's a sadness in his eyes, a weight that seems to burden him with every step.

I want to reach out to him, to offer comfort in whatever troubles him. But I know better than to pry, to push him away with my incessant chatter.

AND I hate him.

So instead, I walk in silence beside him, content to share his company for however long he'll allow it.

"I want to show you my realm," he says, his voice low and measured. I glance at him, surprised.

"Your realm." I echo, curiosity and trepidation in my voice. The sunless sky above is full of ominous clouds swirling, and bats darting through the air, their wings slicing through the stillness.

Nyx nods, his eyes fixed ahead. "It may seem intimidating at first, scary even. But there's a beauty to it," he remarks, his words carrying assurance.

We venture deeper into the forest next to the castle ground. The ominous symphony of thunder and bats takes on a melodic quality, and the play of shadows through the twisted trees becomes a dance with green, silver, and yellow orbs of all shapes and sizes twirling in the air around us as we enter the deep forest. "It's beautiful," I murmur, my eyes absorbing the shifting scenery.

Nyx glances at me, a hint of satisfaction in his expression. "Sometimes, beauty reveals itself in the places least expected," he replies cryptically.

"Is it the same thing for you?" I challenged but he doesn't respond.

The forest floor, adorned with moss and scattered petals, feels plush beneath my feet. The forest becomes even more captivating as we keep walking.

The glowing orbs, suspended in time, drift slowly, they cast a soft, ethereal light that illuminates the entire forest.

I hear the leaves making soft sounds and insects buzzing with every step.

I stop, in awe, as a bunch of tiny bugs, like fireflies, float around, their soft light making the place even more magical.

I giggle when one of them flies right in front of me. To my left, a small pond comes into view, its still waters reflecting the celestial display above. A delicate wooden bridge, adorned with flickering torches, spans the water.

The torchlight's soft glow caresses the pond's surface, creating a play of reflections that adds to the surreal beauty of this place. I stand in shock, soaking in the beauty of this enchanted forest that feels like it's from a dream, not a nightmare.

I take in the breathtaking scene, Nyx steps beside me, his presence tangible, my breath catching in my throat. I feel his body's warmth near mine, making me feel something I didn't want to feel again.

Never.

"Gods, you are the most beautiful things I've ever seen," he remarks, his voice low.

I turn towards him, the reflection of the forest in his almost silver eyes. "It's like a dream, Nyx. I never imagined something so beautiful. Isn't supposed to be the nightmare realm?"

He sighs, "This is the nightmare realm, Aurora. And you should remember that I'm not the gentle one here." He responds with sharpness.

Confused, I furrow my brows. "But... it's not monstrous, it's beautiful and calm, and...you...you made this?"

Nyx takes my hands in his roughly, making me gasp from how tight his grip is on my fingers, I turn to face him. "Yes, but this is different. This is my home. I can create whatever I want."

I look at him, still trying to wrap my head around it all. "I don't understand,"

He gazes into my eyes, a mix of emotions flickering across his face. "I cast in human minds their fear, their trauma, fuck, everything that makes them scarred when they are asleep. I crafted them. But here," He gestures around us, "I create what I want, and sometimes stock some creatures I've already crafted."

"But" I started, but my mouth shut close. I don't know how to ask all the things that spin in my head. Like he can read my mind he yelled, "It's monster you want, Aurora?"

Chapter 18

Aurora

"No…I" He scares me.

Nyx steps back, slowly raising his hands at his sides, an unsettling tremor courses through the forest. The torches and orbs vanish, plunging everything into darkness.

The wind picks up, blowing fiercely through the twisted trees. Nyx's eyes transform, glowing silver-white in the dark, his usually handsome and tortured face now contorted into a malevolent one.

A deep growl resonates, accompanied by the thunderous approach of menacing footsteps to my right.

Panic grips me as I turn, and my eyes widen in terror. A monstrous creature, enormous and horrifying, hurtles toward me with alarming speed.

It's a *big*, creature, standing on four legs. A mix between a bear and a wolf.

It's huge, with fur that's dark and kind of wild.

Its eyes glow red, and it moves fast.

Real fucking fast.

Its red eyes glow menacingly, and the sheer terror of its presence sends chills down my spine. "NYX STOP!" I plead, my voice a frantic plea in the chaotic darkness.

I scramble to the dirt floor, curling into a protective ball, hoping against hope that Nyx will control this beast. The monstrous entity closes in, I can hear it, feel it. "STOP IT, PLEASE," I yelled.

I huddle in fear, thinking the monster is about to get me, but the wind suddenly stops. My hair falls back into place, and I peek from the crook of my elbow to where the monster was standing.

Instead, there's a swarm of glowing white butterflies, soft and silent, twirling in a circle like a tornado.

Still shaking, I extend my arm, tentatively touching the butterflies. I look up at Nyx.

"What the hell was that Nyx?" I snap, anger simmering beneath the surface as I wipe away the last of dirt left on my hands. "You can't just throw monsters at me without a warning!"

Nyx meets my gaze relief and regret in his eyes as they soften. "You had forgotten I was the bad guy, my dear. I needed to remind you."

I stand up straight, crossing my arms. "Well, maybe you could've mentioned that earlier! Instead, I thought I was about to be monster's lunch!"

I glare at him, not ready to let it go. "Next time, a heads-up would be nice. Got it?"

I glance back at the gentle butterflies, their soft glow soothing my nerves.

And with a silent poof of shadows, Nyx disappears.

I'm left standing by the little lake, alone, still shaky.

"Fucker." I grumbled.

"But he made you, you beautiful little creatures." I baby-talk to the glowing butterflies.

Chapter 19

Nyx

)———◇———(

I'm completely utterly *fucked*.

I stand at the entrance of the forest, pacing in endless circles. The air is thick with a maddening energy, and my mind is a chaotic mess. Thoughts of Aurora consume me, and I feel the anger inside me twisting into something darker, something wild.

Gods, I can even see it with the way my shadows burst out of the tips of my fingers.

I'm angry. Not at her, how could I be? But at myself.

I've let my heart take control and now I don't know how I'll make things work.

She looks at me with those eyes – soft, full of understanding as if she sees past the darkness that cloaks my existence.

It infuriates me.

I am not someone to be understood or pitied. I am Nyx, a God, the embodiment of the night, and she has no business unraveling the layers that shield my soul.

Yet, she persists, and it drives me mad. The gentleness in her gaze. I despise the way she makes me feel, the way my thoughts betray me. I want to keep her close, to guard her, own her, eat her, *Gods*, even kill her for the way she makes me feel.

I, who revel in the terror I unleash upon others, find myself ensnared by the innocence reflected in her eyes. It's a contradiction, an unforgivable weakness.

I stop walking and pinch the bridge of my nose roughly, closing my eyelids.

A sigh escapes me and even in the pitch black of my closed eyelids all I see is her.

"Fuck!"

I want to paint the nights of all the men in this universe that had the chance to see her smiled with so much terror that it shatters their fucking being, so much so, that they will wish for death.

And they will find it.

My woman, my smiles.

The forest echoes with the haunting laughter of my delirium as I continue to pace, caught between the harsh feelings inside and the confusing pull of the kindness she sees in me.

Chapter 20

Aurora

)———◇◇———(

Surrounded by white butterflies, yellow and green orbs, and glowing fireflies, I feel like a princess. They look like they like me, whirling around me.

The little creatures dance in the air, making me smile. One playful firefly flutters its wings against my neck, and I can't help but laugh.

I set off along the familiar path that led us here. Surprisingly, all the little creatures decide to follow after me.

"Let's go back," I say softly, urging them on with gentle encouragement.

I walk into the front yard of the castle, and see the chiseled frame of Nyx, standing tall and straight. He looks at me, and it feels like the world stops.

He's so handsome.

His short white hair falling on his forehead makes my lower belly flutter, I don't know why.

But it does.

"Hey!" I call out, waving to him. The butterflies and fireflies continue their dance around me. "Join the fun!" I playfully smile at him while pointing at my new crew.

He takes a step closer. "Enjoying the company of your little friends?" he asks, a smile playing on his lips, his dimples out to charm me too.

I nod happily, "They make everything so gorgeous! And their kind of...you...I mean, you made them."

Nyx's smile deepens, and I can't help but think how perfect this moment is. *Wow, his smile.*

In one swift movement, Nyx is in front of me, grabbing me by the nape of my neck, a forceful grip that sends a little sting of pain through me.

All the little creatures disappear as if they're scared of him. His eyes take on a menacing look, the kind you'd expect from the villain he says he is.

"Already forgot the point I was trying to make in these woods?" he sneers, his voice holding a dark edge.

I tilt my head, trying to lock eyes with him, but it's hard with the way he's holding tightly my neck. "Nope," I reply with a cheeky grin, "but if you want to show me how cruel and bad you can be, there are other ways you can do it."

What is wrong with me?

I want to go home. I want to escape him, why did I just say that?

Why the way he holds me causes my damn pussy to overheat like that.

My heart races, and I know he can feel it, the way his body now presses onto mine leaves no room for me to breathe without pushing on his tight frame.

Nyx's grip tightens, and a wicked smirk plays on his lips. "You think you can handle the darkness, daring?" he taunts, his voice low and rough.

I keep his gaze defiantly, a fire igniting in me. "Try me," I challenge, my tone laced with defiance.

He leans in, his lips dangerously close to my ear. "You have no idea what you're asking for," he growls, the sensation forcing me to close my eyes and open my mouth, a raspy gasp escaping it.

With a wicked glint in his eyes, Nyx releases his hold on my nape, and a surge of relief and disappointment washes over me.

He steps back, but the urge to jump at his throat and bite this damn plumb bottom lip is still very much present.

Nyx smirks, approval in his eyes. "You're playing with fire, Aurora. I was being nice earlier. But my control is fucking thin right now." he warns, his voice dripping with danger and for an unknown reason it made my legs close together in need of some friction.

I take a bold step toward him. I reach out and place a hand on his cheek, but he steps back, elusive.

Not one to back down, I try again, but he continues to evade my touch. This time, I decide to take charge.

I gently cup his face in my hands, but firmly enough that he can't escape me.

Locking eyes with him, I slowly trace a path along his lower lip with my thumbs. His hot breath on my hands makes my blood boil and the inside of my core pulsing.

His mouth closes on my finger, and he bites it, and I moan at the pain. "What are you doing?" he questions, a perplexed expression on his face.

"Affection," I reply, still looking deep into his eyes, "I wanted to touch you."

He makes a strange face, like the idea is distasteful.

I take a step back, ready to respect his boundaries, but he grabs my hands pulling me to him again.

"Do it again," he says, his eyes locking onto mine with an intensity that triggers a chill through my body.

I put my hand flat on his face again. My fingers graze across his skin, feeling the rough texture beneath my touch.

I move towards his closed lips, tracing the outline with a gentle but deliberate pressure. In response, he opens his mouth.

My index slowly enters it, and he presses his body completely with mine, the feel of his hard dick against my belly makes me gasp.

Inhale. Exhale.

The warmth of his tongue envelops my finger as he sucks and licks it.

In the heat of the moment, I decide to explore further, I want him, I want it all.

The dark, the bad, the evil, all of him.

My other hand lowers between us until I grab with my full palm his arousal.

He lets out a low, guttural swear, and without a moment's hesitation, he takes me in his arms, pulling me closer. "Mine."

Our bodies collide, and he crashes his mouth onto mine, a passionate and hungry kiss that leaves me breathless.

Chapter 21

Aurora

We're kissing, wrapped up in each other's arms. He's holding me so tight; that I struggle to expand my chest to breathe. Every touch of his hands on my flesh, or my scalp leaves me seeking more. The world around us fades away. I'm lost.

Lost in his breath.

Lost in his mouth.

"You are made for me," he murmurs, his voice sending heat directly to my clit.

I giggle, "Yours for me,"

He smirks, his eyes gleaming with a mischievous glint. "I've got more surprises for you, my dear."

I tilt my head and look at Nyx, my eyes wide and filled with questions.

He grins at me and says, "Hold tight."

Before I can react, his eyes start to glow, and we're not on solid ground anymore.

Lying on my back, I feel the cool surface beneath me, unsure of where exactly I am. The world is a swirl of confusion, but simultaneously, I'm aware of being in the air.

The wind rushes past with a forceful push, tousling my hair and carrying the scent of something humid.

It's a disorienting yet invigorating sensation and I've never felt more alive.

"What the fuck?" I gasp, taking in the strange surroundings.

Nyx grins, his gaze filled with desire. "We're on a dragon, darling."

I gawk at the majestic creature beneath us. "A dragon? Seriously?"

Nyx nods, his hands running down my sides. "Surprised?"

I laugh nervously, "Uh, yeah! But it's amazing!"

The dragon lets out a low, rumbling growl, and I realize we're flying through the sky. The rush of wind is exhilarating.

"This is insane!" I shout over the wind, a mix of excitement and fear in my voice.

"When I found you in the library, asleep. I saw that you were reading a book mentioning the ancient Umbrosus.

I thought you would like to see something that comes as close as possible, as they are extinct."

Nyx leans in, his lips brushing against mine, and I dare use the tip of my tongue to lick his bottom lip. "Get ready for a ride, my love. Because I'll fuck this perfect cunt of yours on this dragon."

Nyx fastens his belt; his movements are swift and purposeful, raw, and hungry. I can't tear my eyes away, licking my lips and biting on the inside of my cheek, until I taste the coppery tang.

His gaze meets mine, intense and penetrating, like a predator ready to pounce. There's something primal and untamed about him that both scares and excites me.

Lying on my back, the wind rushing past me as the dragon soars high in the sky.

Nyx positions himself close to my core, between my legs. He frees himself, and his impressive length springs free, causing my eyes to widen.

He's really big down there.

He grabs it so hard that the pink tip changes color then rolls his head from side to side while looking at me.

"If I were you, I would grab onto anything. Because, darling, I won't be gentle," he croons.

Nyx is rough, unapologetic, and crude. But there's something about the way he carries himself that stirs something inside me. I've never felt this way before for someone. For any men.

He leans over me, and I smile seductively. Frantically searching for something to hold on to, afraid that I might fall, I try to grab onto anything without looking somewhere else.

I know he might let me fall. He's a god. He's incapable of feeling more than desire and lust.

I steady myself by pushing my fingers under the dragon's sharp scales, cutting myself in the process.

"Ouch." The pain makes me gasp, but I hold on, determined not to let go.

The wind tugs at my hair, and I close my eyes for a moment, letting the sensation wash over me. In this moment, high above the earth, with Nyx and the dragon, I feel freedom.

"Did you hurt yourself, my love?" Nyx asked, grabbing the hem of my dress, and tugging strongly one time, making it crack with the sound of ripping tissue. Leaving me exposed to the cold air and naked.

He's smiling at me and starts rubbing the tip of his dick all along my soaking-wet entrance.

"Y... yes." I managed.

I open my eyes again, meeting Nyx's silver-blue ones. He standing straight as the god he is.

The dragon's powerful wings beat against the air, and the rush of adrenaline adds to the intoxicating sensation. It's a mix of danger and exhilaration that leaves me breathless.

He teases my entrance with the tip, and starts pushing its way inside, entering so slowly it's almost painful. I gasp at the sensation, caught between pleasure and agony.

He stops when an inch is in, now his face a breath away from mine. He grabs my arm roughly and brings my hands in front of his face, between the two of us.

The blood from the cut on my finger drips on my face and chest. He growls, closes his eyes, and brings his face close to my fingers.

Our eyes lock. "I want to taste every part of you, feel you squirm under my touch," he murmurs, his voice dirty, husky and so fucking arousing makes me squirm underneath him in need.

He sucks on my finger so hard it stings the injury, and I let out a gasp, a mixture of pleasure and pain. The intensity of the moment overwhelms me.

"I want all of you," he says, gripping my wrist even tighter before pushing my fingers deep into his throat, causing him to drool a mix of his saliva and my blood onto me.

It's nasty. Animal. But powerful.

I open my mouth, tasting the mix dripping from him, and he moans, looking at me.

"Look at you, *dirty, dirty*, just for me," he sings in my ear.

His mouth drops just below my jaw and bites on the soft flesh, causing my eyes to widen and let a cry-like moan escape me.

He enters me completely with one furious thrust, and I'm submerged in all the sensations. "Fuck," I breathe. Nyx laughs, and his warm breath tickles my cheek. He licks the side of my face with a large tongue. "Oh," He mocked. "Did I hurt you, darling?"

I try to answer, but then he moves and thrusts again, so deep, that our pubic bones crash together, making my head spin and my eyes roll.

I grab his hair tightly, almost tearing his scalp, and bring his face to mine. He looks surprised, but I muster the strength to say, "No." And then he loses it, pounding hard, *really hard.*

I replace my hands behind my head, pushing them under the scales again, feeling the cut puncture my skin again. Our bodies move in sync, the dragon's powerful wings beating against the wind.

As much as I want to deny it, there's a part of me that longs for this connection.

Chapter 22

She's perfect, and I can't let her go.

She'll stay here until her mortal bodies give up.

I'm fucking her, and she has the guts to look me in the eyes and provoke me. It makes me want to push it farther.

I stop, freeing myself with a wet pop, looking down at her red dripping cunt.

I slap her pussy hard with my hand. "You like that?" I ask her, knowing she does.

She looks at me, and I take her face in my hand so hard it will probably leave a mark. *Good.*

I crook my head and look her in the eyes. "You should be scared."

Then I twist her, and she yells in horror as I position her on her belly, facing the void, dangling from the dragon's side.

My fucking puppet.

I crush my body on top of her and start fucking her from behind. "Gods, Aurora."

She moans and screams, but that only makes me want her more.

"I'll fuck this ass of mine son if you don't fall." I lose myself in the rhythm of her panicking, trying to back up.

Consumed by the desire to possess her completely, I'm mad. I'm doomed. She got me now. Heart and soul.

"Come for me, my dear," I growl, gripping more tightly her hips. She is close, I feel it, I feel the walls of her sacred pussy trying to milk me, spasming on my sensitive dick.

"Oh my…fuck. Nyx." She yelled, breathless.

"I know, love," I answer. "Come now. Aurora."

And she does, fucking heaven.

I explode with her, cuming all inside her. She's riding the wave, grinding on me, and it's the most beautiful thing I've ever seen.

Her round ass pushing on me like that, makes me want to bite into it.

When she's done, I tug on her arms to help her sit in front of me, her face red from the climax and the surplus of blood in her head.

She looks at me with those mesmerizing eyes and whispers, "This was the best sex I've ever had." My heart swells with something feeling like joy, and *that,* won't do.

Smiling at her, I wink and push her. Making her fall from the dragon.

I watch her gracefully tumble through the air, her yells echoing in the eternal night.

Chapter 23

Aurora

)———◇———(

A week later

It's been a week since the crazy fuck session with Nyx on the dragon. This was insane, like him. But he got all mad, *for I don't fucking know.* And threw me off which, really pissed me off.

One moment I'm up high, feeling amazing, and the next, I'm plummeting down, thinking I'm gonna die.

But, of course, Nyx caught me in the air, like nothing happened, took me back to the castle, and dropped me on the floor in front of the door. *Fucker.*

Since then, I've locked myself in my room, and I haven't come out. I'm still super mad at him for this, especially because he just entered the castle without talking to me after and left me with my shaking legs and my questions.

He sent food and little notes, but I only ate the food. The notes went straight into the trash can.

I'm sitting on the floor, staring out the window, lost in my thoughts. A sudden knock disrupts my solitude, and I glance towards the door. Frowning, I call out, "Go away, Nyx. I'm not interested unless it's a grand entrance with bubbles to announce me I'm going home."

"Open the door, Aurora. I've had enough of your tantrum. If you don't, I'll come in anyway."

My frustration grows, and I retort, "I don't want to see you right now. Just leave me alone."

His voice takes on a stern edge, "This is your last chance. Open the door, or I'm coming in."

I roll my eyes, muttering a curse under my breath, and decide to stay sit. The air is still, and the only sound is the soft hum of my breathing now.

Suddenly, the tranquility shatters as the door bursts open with a jarring breaking sound. My head whips around to see Nyx on the other side, his dark brows knitted together, casting shadows over his intense eyes that flicker with an angry fire and his silver glow.

The lines on his forehead deepen, and his jaw clenches, emphasizing the tension in his face. The atmosphere crackles with the electricity

"WHAT ARE YOU…" Just as I'm about to holler and lose my shit, multicolored bubbles, begin to drop from the ceiling.

I froze, incapable of stopping watching the amazing way they move.

I open my hands, palms up, in front of me, embracing the whimsical display of slowly falling effervescent spheres, each one a vibrant hue.

The room is transformed into a magical haven, the colors reflecting off the walls with the candlelight glow.

Even though Nyx came in all grumpy, breaking the door, the pretty bubbles made me feel a bit better.

How can I don't?

I stay still on the floor, completely mesmerized. They're floating around me, and I can't help but smile as I reach out to touch them.

Pop!

One bursts at my fingertips.

I glance up, and there's Nyx, this towering figure, looking at me with one of his dimples showing a bit more than usual.

I grin up at him, "Hey, you should try popping these. It's kind of fun!"

Nyx raises an eyebrow, a hint of a smile playing on his lips, "Fun? I doubt it."

I giggle, "Come on, just try it."

He sighs but bends down, popping one with his long finger. I burst into laughter, "See? It's not that bad, right?"

"You asked for them," he responds.

"Aurora, why have you been ignoring me for a week?" He asks, and he's looking sad, panicking, stressed, perhaps.

I roll my eyes, "I haven't been ignoring you. Just busy."

He frowns, "Busy with the dust? Look, I picked you up after tossing you off that dragon. What more do you want?" he retorts, irritation clear in his voice.

I cross my arms, giving him some attitude, "Well, maybe not throwing me off a dragon would be a start."

He sighs, "Is that all?"

"I don't know. Maybe sending me back home?"

"Not happening." He grinned deviously, his eyes gleaming with mischief

I huff, and he grabs my wrist and coldly says, "Follow me. I've got a surprise for you."

I raise an eyebrow but follow as he leads the way.

Chapter 24

I walk through the castle with Aurora at my side, our fingers entwined. It's a strange sensation, one I'm not entirely comfortable with. I don't know if I love the way it makes my heart feel fuller.

But I fucking can't help but squeeze her hand a little tighter. She returns the gesture, and for a moment, the world outside fades away all importance, time, hate, and history. Just *her*.

I felt bad for throwing her off the dragon's back. But I needed to remind her I was not the good guy in her story. I'm her *kidnapper*, I'm the reason she's having terrible nightmares every night for one year now. So, I decided to plan something for her, because I want those pretty smiles.

I move behind her and place my hand on her face, hiding her beautiful blue eyes. "I've got something for you," I announce.

"Again?" She jumps.

I bite my lips, not bothering to hide my full-on grin since she can't see it.

"Yes."

Leading the way through the castle, I guide her by pushing on her hips with my body, her feet following the push of mine.

Eventually, we reach the kitchen. I remove my hands from her face, and she opens her eyes to find a spread of various ingredients and utensils. The surprise is written all over her face – joy and gratitude illuminating her features.

"I thought you might miss baking," I say, my voice softer than usual. The water glistening in her eyes doesn't spill over, but her smile tells me I've succeeded in bringing a spark of happiness to her.

She gasps and brings her hands in front of her mouth before starting to walk toward the big black stone kitchen island.

She looks at the array of baking supplies. "Nyx, this is amazing! How did you know I missed baking?"

I smirk, "I have my ways of figuring things out. Thought it might be something you'd enjoy."

Her smile widens, she starts running in my direction and throws her arms around me. "Thank you, this is the sweetest thing anyone's ever done for me."

I pat her back awkwardly, not entirely used to these displays of affection. "Well, don't get too mushy on me. Let's see what you can whip up with all this."

She steps back, "Yes, Chef Nyx. Your wish is my command."

I chuckle, "Just bake something good."

She begins to gather ingredients, the kitchen coming alive with the sound of her humming and the clatter of utensils.

I watch her, still puzzled by the unfamiliar warmth I feel. Maybe this surprise wasn't just for her; maybe it was for me too, I think.

Aurora's excitement echoes through the kitchen as she jumps up and down like an overjoyed child. Then, she stops moving. I tilted my head slightly to the side, furrowing my brows in confusion.

She delicately brings one of the spoons up in the air above her head. Looking at it like it's some sacred relics.

She exclaims, "NO, YOU DID NOT!"

The spoon is a comical sight, adorned with a vibrant yellow color and small pink cherries.

Aurora stares at it in disbelief, her eyes wide with amazement. "Where did this come from?" she asks, still marveling at the spoon.

I explain, "Well, gods can't interact directly with humans in their world, as I explained, but just like we can bring people into our realm, we can also do it with objects. It's a bit trickier, but clearly not impossible." I lean against the kitchen counter, observing her with a bemused expression.

The joy on her face is worth every bit of effort put into this surprise.

Chapter 25

)———◇◇◇———(

As Aurora continues to bake, I find myself drawn to her movements, the way she gracefully measures out ingredients and expertly mixes them. She insisted that I join her, despite my protests that I've never done any baking before. After all, as a God, my food simply appears at my command.

With a growl of annoyance, I finally give in and stand beside her, watching her work with a mix of fascination and amusement. Unable to resist, I wrap my arms around her from behind, planting kisses along her neck and biting gently.

She chuckles, squirming slightly in my embrace. "You know, I could still hold a grudge against you for throwing me off that dragon, the beast in the woods, and kidnapping me," she teases, turning to face me.

I raise an eyebrow, feigning innocence. "And yet here we are."

A mischievous glint sparkles in her eyes as she dips her finger into a bowl of flour and starts drawing patterns on my face. I let her, enjoying the feel of her touch and the sound of her laughter.

She bites her lip in concentration, and I admire the way her nose wrinkles when she focuses intently on a task.

How a human could be so perfect?

I always thought of them as spineless scarred little creatures. The memory of my forced assignment as the God of Nightmares comes to my mind feeling my smile disappear from my lips

I never got the chance to choose my path like other gods. It was thrust upon me by the king of gods himself, simply because my father held the title before me. It is he who assigns the titles and domains to the newly ascended gods, ensuring the balance and order of our world.

Morphea and I had always dreamed of swapping roles; I longed for the Reveries realm, while she coveted Nightmares.

But fate had other plans.

Now, I find myself in a realm I never wanted, tasked with casting terror that plagues humanity with their fears. However, I've tried to twist my role into something less sinister, aiming to aid rather than torment.

Yet, Aurora... She's a puzzle. Beneath her gentle exterior lies a strength I've rarely encountered. Her resilience is undeniable, and it draws me in.

The gods are beings of immense power, each ruling over their domain within the vast expanse of the

Godsland. Each god possesses unique abilities and responsibilities that can't be exchanged with others when assigned.

I wish it was different.

Aurora's spontaneous kiss pulls me out of my thoughts, her lips brushing against mine briefly before she speaks. "Finish," she says with a proudness.

Intrigued by her words, I conjure a mirror into my hands and gaze into it. Aurora chuckles beside me as I examine my face.

I look at my reflection, feeling surprise at the sight before me. Little hearts and butterflies adorn my features, and a big smile has been drawn across my face.

Aurora bursts into laughter beside me, the sound echoing through the room. A sigh escapes my lips. "What have you done?" I ask, unable to hide the hint of entertainment in my voice.

She grins playfully, her eyes sparkling with naughtiness. "Just adding to your charm," she replies, her tone playful.

I chuckle at her response, despite my initial reluctance to include her antics. "So, you find me charming," I asked, unable to resist the smile that tugged at my lips.

Aurora laughs again, her joy contagious as she reaches out to touch my cheek. "Yes. But now, you look adorable," she says, her voice filled with genuine affection.

I roll my eyes playfully; I can't deny the warmth that spreads through me at her words. "I'll have you know, I am a god of nightmares, and I can kill you with a snap of the fingers," I tease, unable to resist the opportunity to threaten her.

She giggles, leaning in to press a quick kiss to my cheek. "Even gods need a little cheer sometimes," she says softly.

I smile at her words, grateful for her presence in my life.

She'll never leave me.

Chapter 26

)———◇◇◇———(

Nyx finishes the last bite of the muffin I made, and I am so proud to see his face soften as he swallows. "So, what did you think?" I ask eagerly.

He nods appreciatively, a small smirk playing on his lips. "Delicious," he replies, his voice carrying a warmth that makes my heart flutter.

Aurora. You can't fall for him.

Too late.

Grinning, I take a sip of my tea before going into the topic that's been on my mind. "You know, I was flipping through a book the other day and came across something interesting," I begin, my curiosity piquing.

"It was a picture of a black lotus. Have you ever seen one in real life? They sound so intriguing, don't they? I wonder if they're as beautiful as they're described."

Nyx's expression grows thoughtful as he considers my question. "I've heard of them," he replies suspiciously, his gaze distant as if lost in memory. "But they have been all burned by Vion. They are strictly prohibited."

I lean forward, eager for more information. "What do they look like? Are they really black? And yeah, I read that it's because it can change or play with powers isn't?" I insist.

Nyx nods, a faint smile ghosting his plump lips. "Yes, they're black, but not in the way you might think. Their petals have a velvety texture, almost like the night sky," he explains, his voice taking on a dreamy quality. "And when they bloom under the moonlight, they shimmer with an otherworldly beauty. Some legends, but they were before I was even born, centuries ago, implied them to be a source of power for the ancient gods, the *Originel*. Making them more powerful. Some of them used it to change their appearance and trick the other gods. So, Vion decided to banish them."

I sigh with longing, picturing the beauty of such a magical flower. "That sounds enchanting," I murmur, lost in Nyx's description.

He chuckles softly, his eyes gleaming with amusement. "Maybe there's still one around for you to see," he suggests and winks at me.

The thought fills me with anticipation. "I'd love that," I respond, feeling my heart swell with thrill.

Suddenly, Nyx stands up, grabs my hand, and pulls me away. I gasp in surprise, my heart racing.

Before I can comprehend what's happening, he squeezes me in his arms, close to his body and we vanish.

When I open my eyes again, I'm standing outside on a hill, overlooking the same stone bridges I first saw when I arrived. But Nyx is gone, and a wave of worry washes over me. me. "Nyx?" I call out tentatively, my voice echoing through the stillness of the forest.

I hear his voice in response, but it sounds distant as if coming from far away. Determined to find him, I start walking, my nerves tingling with anticipation as I venture deeper into the woods.

The trees loom overhead, their branches reaching out like skeletal fingers, casting shadows on the forest floor. But I push forward, my determination outweighing my fear, until finally, I spot him.

He is kneeling next to a bush, his expression one of awe as he gazes at something hidden within. Curious, I approach him, the sound of my heart so loud in my ears I catch sight of what has captured his attention.

There, nestled among the lush vegetation and twisting vines, is a real black lotus. Its petals are as dark as midnight, contrasting starkly against the vibrant greenery surrounding it. I gasp in wonder, unable to tear my eyes away from its mesmerizing beauty.

Nyx looks up at me, a smile playing on his lips as he sees my reaction. "I thought you might like to see one up close," he says tenderly, his voice filled with warmth.

I nod, feeling a surge of gratitude towards him for sharing this secret with me. "Nyx," I reply, my voice barely above a whisper as I reach out to touch the delicate petals of the flower. "It's beautiful,"

I close the distance with the plant, and I'm amazed by the long, menacing thorns that protrude from its stem. I turn to Nyx with a furrowed brow. "Is it true?" I ask, my voice barely above a whisper.

Nyx hesitates for a moment before answering, his expression troubled. "I don't know," he admits, his voice tinged with sadness.

"Why haven't you tried?" I add, unable to hide the judgment in my voice.

A shadow crosses Nyx's face, and he looks away, his gaze distant. "I don't want anything to do with more power," he confesses quietly. "I just wanted to live my way to the end of my word duties, doing my best, and fuck you endlessly."

Not so cold anymore. I think to myself.

Without hesitation, I reach out and cup his face in my hands, my fingers gently tracing the contours of his jaw. Leaning in, I press my lips to his, pouring all of my love and support into the kiss. "That's... so sad," I quietly say against his lips, my voice trembling with emotion. "You deserve so much more."

Nyx takes a deep breath. "Long, long ago," he begins, his voice carrying the weight of centuries. "At the beginning of humankind, The God of death grew rebellious. He sought to change the order of things, to gain power and challenge the king of gods."

I listen intently, my heart heavy with the weight of his words.

"He attempted to use the black lotus to achieve his goals," Nyx continues, his voice tinged with a hint of fear. "But he failed. The lotus was too powerful and unpredictable, and he was caught before he could use it. Vion destroyed the trees and the God too."

A shiver runs down my spine.

Nyx's expression darkens. "I've always been afraid of that damn plant," he admits, his voice barely above a whisper. "But my mother... she loved their beauty. She would often read about them in books and longed to see one in person."

He pauses, a bittersweet smile tugging at the corners of his lips. "So, I searched the entire realm, and even the paradise realm when I had the chance on the two celebrations each year. And one day, I found it."

My eyes widen in astonishment as I realize the lengths Nyx went to for his mother's happiness.

Definitely not so cold.

"I found a baby black lotus," Nyx continues, his voice soft with nostalgia. "And I surprised my mother with it. She was overjoyed." He falls silent, lost in memories of a time long past.

I reach out and take his hand in mine, squeezing it gently in silent understanding. Despite the fear and uncertainty that surrounds the black lotus, there is also a sense of love and devotion that binds Nyx to it.

Nyx's grip my face, his touch both forceful and electrifying. A surge of arousal courses through me, my sex pulsing with desire at his strong presence.

Maybe, just maybe. I can stay with him. Leaving all my past, and problems behind?

"We're done talking about it," he declares, his voice low and commanding.

I bite my lip, a rush of excitement flooding my senses. "What do you want to do?" I ask breathlessly.

He looks at me with a predatory gaze, his eyes smoldering with desire. "I want you," he says huskily, his words dripping with raw sensuality.

My heart races at his words, my body responding eagerly to him. Without hesitation, I grab onto him, feeling the now, familiar sensation of teleportation surrounding me.

In an instant, we're in his room, his lips on mine. I know what's coming next, and I can't wait to lose myself in us.

I can't wait to forget.

I can't wait to touch him.

I can't wait to *feel*.

Chapter 27

Aurora

I feel my body being thrown onto a bed. I look around the room. It's dark, but the flickering light of a hundred candles brings a sultry atmosphere. It's the first time I've seen Nyx's room, and there's something about it that feels even more sensual.

The walls are all black, but crimson drapes fall from the ceiling, adding a vibe to this room that I love.

I use my elbow to up my body as he walks to the foot of the bed. He slowly undresses in front of me, his eyes never leaving mine.

I can't help but look at his body, feeling a tingle in my stomach. "Like what you see, my love?" Nyx's voice is low and husky.

I nod, unable to find my voice. I've never felt this kind of desire before, and it's both thrilling and scary.

Because I have no control. I can't do anything. He could ask me to eat my own shit and I'll gladly do it.

That's a dangerous game.

Nyx leans in closer, his breath warm on the skin of my cleavage. "You're so beautiful, Aurora," he whispers, his fingers trailing down my arm. I close my eyes at his touch, feeling a wave of longing wash over me.

I watch as he leans back, his eyes never leaving my body. "Do you trust me, Aurora?" he asks, his tone filled with sincerity.

I hesitate for a moment. *Do I?*

I agree with a quick shake of my head, a sense of surrender washing over me.

I need him, I need him to touch me.

Nyx's lips curl into a tantalizing smile as

He edges nearer completely nude and so…so…*hard.*

He's looking at me with that intense gaze that tells me he wants to devour me whole.

I fucking hope he did.

I awkwardly start to remove all my clothes, feeling his eyes on me the entire time.

He just waits, watching me with a hunger that sends my mind spiraling, I literally need to remind myself to breathe.

He wants to claim me and possess me, and I think I will let him do it.

"So beautiful." He murmurs. His words make me feel seen and desired. "You are exquisite," he purred, kissing my forehead before trailing down, leaving a trail of wet kisses in its path. Every touch feels like an electric shock directly to my clit.

He worships me with his hands and lips. "You are a goddess," he whispers, his voice like a soft, as his mouth reaches my belly button.

I can't help but let out a soft moan as his hands reach between my legs, sending waves of heat through my whole body.

"Let go, Aurora," he murmurs, his breath warm against my skin. "Let everything go, let me love you."

I close my eyes and surrender to the sensation of his breath catching on the sensitive flesh of my pussy.

The feeling of his two hands spreading my lips in two makes me suddenly gasp. "You are a revelation," he whispers, his eyes fixated between my legs, looking at my spread cunt, seeing parts of me that I haven't even discovered myself.

At that moment, I realize that something has shifted between us. It's not just about physical attraction; there's a deeper connection that's forming, one that I feel in the depths of my soul.

I can't leave him.

One of his fingers starts gliding along me, making me moan. "Fuck."

He breathes roughly. "Look at that glistening cunt. You love it when I touch you like that, darling?"

"Yes." I deadpan.

"Well, you're in for a treat, because I'm about to fucking worship you whole for the rest of your mortal life, my love." He laughs.

And with that, he dived, covering all of my vulva in his mouth. Aspiring, licking, eating it like he's life depends on it.

"Oh, wow." I'm speechless, grabbing the sheets with white knuckles, moving my hips to grind on his damn pretty face.

"Don't…stop," I mumble.

With a growl that makes my clit vibrate he speaks, his mouth surrounding my intimate parts. "Never."

Chapter 28

Aurora

───◇◇◇───

"I want you to fuck me," I whisper, my voice barely above a breath.

Nyx's eyes darken with desire, and a smirk tugs at the corners of his lips. "I love hearing that," he mumbles, his voice low and gravely.

I feel a thrill run through me at his words, and I smile back at him. "There's something else I want," I say, my heart pounding in my chest.

Nyx raises an eyebrow in curiosity. "What do you want?" he asks, his voice fills with curiosity.

"I want you to leash me," I say, feeling a blush creep up my cheeks.

A slow grin spreads across Nyx's face, and with a flick of his wrist, a leather collar appears around my neck. The tightness of it against my skin automatically makes it hard to breathe, the weight of the chains in his hand pulling my head to the side.

I look up at Nyx. "I knew you were a dark one, my love." He speaks.

His gaze grows serious as he pulls gently on the leash, guiding me to get up on my knees and closer to him. "Now," he says, his voice low and commanding, "you belong to me."

Nyx gets up from the bed, his hardness proudly pointing at me. He tugs hard the chain, forcing the collar to pull my head to the front, I fall onto my hands and crawl towards him on all fours.

On my hands and knees, I slowly make my way to him. Every movement is deliberate, and sensual, swinging my hips up in the air.

I feel the intensity of his eyes on me, burning with desire, it's almost tangible, hurting even.

Stopping in front of his dick, without breaking eye contact, I lick the tip of it. Making a circle around it, tasting the bead of pre cum, savoring the taste of him.

"My love. My Goddess." He crooned between grith teeth.

"Fuck me, Nyx," I respond with confidence.

With a firm grip on my hair, Nyx yanks me down to the floor, and I land on my face with a thud.

Before I can react, he enters me with one powerful thrust from behind, eliciting a mixture of yells and growls from my lips.

I'm overwhelmed by the feel of him, pinned to the floor beneath him.

His hand presses against the side of my face, holding me in place as he continues to ravish me.

I catch sight of one of his fingers dangling in front of me, and without hesitation, I bite down on it with all my force. The sensation seems to turn him on even more, he moans at the pain. We are grunting, moaning, swearing. *It's ugly.*

It's raw.

It's powerful.

It's us.

As my climax reaches its peak, I feel Nyx's release synchronize with mine, our bodies quivering together.

With a final shaky trust, he stops moving. "Fuck." He hardly murmurs.

He leans down next to me on the floor, his touch gentle as he uses his magic to make the collar and chain disappear.

With a tender expression, he begins stroking my hair with care, his fingers trailing soothingly along my scalp. "You're incredible," he murmurs, his voice filled with a mixture of admiration and *love.*

I smile up at him, feeling a warmth spreading through me at his touch. "And you're not so bad yourself for a cold asshole," I tease, my tone laced with affection.

He chuckles softly.

This damn sound is becoming my favorite.

His eyes lock with mine. "My fearless love," he says, his gaze softening as he continues to stroke my hair.

I lean into his touch, feeling contentment wash over me. "You love me, don't you?" I whisper.

I turn my head to look into his eyes, finding a vulnerability there that touches my heart. "You mean everything to me, Aurora," he begins, his voice soft but filled with conviction. "Since the moment I laid eyes on you, you've captured my heart in a way I never thought possible. You're not just a fleeting infatuation or a passing fancy. You're the one who completes me, who makes me whole. I've broken all the rules by stalking your sleep, stopping Morphea from letting you dream and taking you to this cursed realm. But just for touching you again, I would do it all over again. I would damn my soul for a chance at seeing you smile again."

I listen, captivated by his words, feeling my own emotions welling up inside me. "Nyx..." I murmur, my voice barely above a breath.

He reaches out to cup my face gently in his calloused hands, his touch warm against my skin. "I love you more than words can express," he continues, his gaze never wavering from mine. "With you, I feel alive in ways I never knew I could."

Tears prick at the corners of my eyes as I listen to him pour out his heart to me, his words wrapping around me like a comforting embrace.

I breathe deeply, not allowing myself to cry. "I love you too," I finally manage to say, my voice filled with emotion. "With all my heart and soul."

He smiles, a radiant expression that lights up his features. "Together, we'll conquer any obstacle," he vows, his voice brimming with determination.

And in that moment, as we hold each other close, I know that we're destined to be together, bound by a love that transcends everything.

Chapter 29

I watch Aurora sleeping peacefully in my bed, her soft breathing calms me. Here, at this moment, she is free from the torment of her nightmares, shielded from the haunting memories that plague her when she sleeps.

It's a relief to see her like this, undisturbed and at peace.

I find myself reflecting on the countless women who have passed through my bed over the years, none of whom I have ever allowed to stay for more than a fleeting encounter.

But with Aurora, it's different.

Fuck, it's so different.

There's something about her presence that fills my existence with light, something that makes me want to keep her close, to protect her.

Aurora stirs and wakes up, her eyes automatically finding mine, and I'm captivated by the depth of emotion I see reflected in those blue orbs.

"Good morning, darling," I whisper, reaching out to brush a strand of hair from her face.

"Morning," she mumbles, her voice soft and sleepy. "What are you thinking about?"

I hesitate for a moment before deciding to broach the subject that has been weighing on my mind. "I was wondering... What are your nightmares about?"

Her expression turns serious as she considers my question, I see the pain in her eyes, and it pisses me off.

"When I was eight years old," she begins, her voice trembling slightly, "my family and I were walking on a frozen lake. We were happy, laughing... But then there was an accident. The ice cracked and we plunged into the cold water."

I listen in silence as she recounts the harrowing

events of that night, feeling a lump form in my throat as she describes this day.

"I remember the strong current, tossing us in all directions, unable to find the hole through which we had fallen. My sister and I were crying, screaming for help, filling our laughs with water. My dad wasn't responding, he was floating away, eyes closed, and my mom was frantic, trying to swim to us. She managed to grab my sister by the waist and come to join me. She found a hole... but it was far away. I had more resistance than they did, she looked at me, and pushed me with all her might towards the exit..."

Aurora's voice falters as she recalls the story and I almost stop her, seeing her like that, seeing her on the verge of crying, it breaks me.

"My mom... she always told me when I was scared, you'll not fear. And I swear I think she said it before pushing me. I watched as she sank deep into the water with my sister."

Tears well up in Aurora's eyes as she relives the traumatic memory, and I reach out to hold her.

"I'm sorry, Aurora," I whisper, my soul

breaking for her. I put her through this, each night for a fucking year.

I'm a monster.

She nods, grateful for my understanding.

"You're so fucking strong, Aurora," I whisper, my voice choked with emotion. "Not a single tear on your face, even after everything you've been through."

She looks up at me, her eyes shimmering with unshed tears. "I cried enough," she replies, her voice trembling slightly.

I lay myself completely on my back, and pull her close, wrapping my arms around her tightly as if to shield her from the pain of the past.

"I'm sorry," I murmur, pressing a gentle kiss to the top of her head. "I wish I could take away all your pain, make it disappear forever."

She rests her head against my chest, her breath warm against my skin, and for a moment, we simply hold each other in silence.

"It's okay, Nyx," she says, her voice barely above a whisper. "Just having you here with me... It's enough."

I feel a pang of guilt wash over me at her words, knowing that I'm responsible for so much of her suffering.

All I can do is plant a kiss on the top of her head, taking in the scent of her.

"You'll never be alone, Aurora," I whisper, my voice barely audible. "I'll always be here."

Chapter 30

Two weeks later

It's been two weeks since I confessed to Nyx, and since then, I've been on a rollercoaster of emotions. Anger, sadness, confusion... But now, I finally feel at peace.

I fucking miss Meya.

But I'm ok with my decision to stay here. I've made my peace with it.

I'm flipping through pages of ancient legends, delving into tales of powerful beings and long-forgotten gods. The *Originels*.

Nyx's cold ways may be intimidating to some, but I've grown to love it. His grumpy attitude somehow makes me feel drawn to him. He's real.

Even though he may seem tough on the outside, I know there's a kind heart inside him.

I gaze without really concentrating on the pages of the big book on my thighs, I let my fingers slide on the paper. Feeling its texture. The title is written in large, beautiful black letters.

Death Realm

It is written that the last deity in charge was an Originel. But this one has gone mad and now it is the king of the gods who takes care of gathering the dying human souls and carrying their souls to the right place.

The death god died long ago, two generations of gods. I sigh.

So like 2000 years?

I turn the page and immediately my gaze catches the name of Vion.

This fucker has been the king since the creation, so he's the last one that ever seen this realm operative not by his hand.

I've asked questions about him to Nyx. And he described him as, a loner god, not participating in celebrations nor speaking to anyone.

He grew bored.

I sense a presence beside me and quickly jerk my head, Nyx leans against the doorframe, his presence filling the doorway. "Aurora," he says in his deep voice, "come to our room. You need to prepare yourself."

I look up from the book, curiosity filling my belly. "Why do I need to prepare myself?" I ask, unable to hide the excitement in my voice.

He smirks a glint of mischief in his eyes. "You'll see," he replies cryptically, his gaze lingering on me for a moment longer than necessary.

My heart skips a beat as I take in his appearance. He looks stunning, dressed all in black with red lace details on his shirt. His hair is slicked back, giving him a dangerous yet handsome look.

Damn, he's handsome.

"What are you up to," I ask playfully, already feeling the anticipation building inside me as I get up from the chair and jump towards him.

He chuckles softly, "You'll find out soon enough," he says.

We enter the room; my eyes widen in amazement at the sight before me. There, laid out on the bed, is a magnificent black gown. It's sleek and elegant, with intricate crimson lace detailing shimmering in the candlelight matching the one on his shirt. The fabric drapes beautifully, and I can't help but imagine how it will feel against my skin.

And wait… There's a panty!

"What the hell? A panty" I laugh.

"Yes. I didn't want to, but I thought you would like to gesture. You can choose not to wear it though." He responds with a wink.

I turn to Nyx, a mix of emotions written across my face. "Wow, this is stunning," I exclaim, unable to contain my excitement. "But why? What's the occasion?"

Nyx simply smiles enigmatically, his eyes gleaming with mischief. "It's the *Bonum Day*, the paradise realm celebrates all the new souls of the past year," he replies. "Go on, try it on."

I nod excitedly, unable to resist the beauty of the dress. With shaky hands, I touch the fabric, feeling its softness under my fingertips.

The bedroom is so quiet, and Nyx is just staring at me as I take off my clothes. It feels like there's this heavy tension hanging in the air.

I slip into the dress, and Nyx comes over to me. "Need some help there?" he asks, his voice low and husky.

"Yeah, could you?" I reply, trying to keep my own voice steady.

He steps closer, and the feel of the warmth of his fingers as he reaches around me to work on the laces makes me close my eyes. His touch is gentle, but there's this roughness lingering not too deep, I can feel it.

"Thanks," I mumble, feeling my cheeks heat up.

"No problem," he says, his breath brushing against my neck.

We stand there for a moment, just breathing each other in. It's like time has stopped, and all that exists is this moment between us.

"Are you ready?" he finally asks, his voice breaking the silence.

"I think so," I say, my heart racing.

He steps back, and I turn to face him, feeling a little breathless. We look at each other for a long moment, and I can see something in his eyes that makes my stomach flip.

"You look amazing," he says softly, his voice filled with sincerity.

"Thanks," I reply, feeling a blush spread across my cheeks. We stay like that for a moment, just smiling at each other, the tension between us almost palpable.

"Shall we go?" he asks, holding out his hand.

"Yeah," I say, taking it without hesitation.

We leave the room together, I can't help but feel like maybe, *just maybe*, I'm already so knee-deep in love.

Chapter 31

Aurora

"Yay, we're going to a party in the paradise realm! WHOOP WHOOP," I squeal with excitement as Nyx and I stroll outside the castle. I glance down at the black high heels he gave me just before we step outside. "Um, these heels are a bit tricky on this dirt road," I admit, trying not to wobble too much.

Nyx chuckles, "You'll get used to them. We're walking to the party."

"Walking?" I pout, my excitement deflating a bit. "Not flying, teleporting, or, uh, magical horses?"

He sighs, clearly a bit exasperated. "No, just walking. It's not that far, and I thought you might enjoy the journey."

"Oh, okay," I say, a tad disappointed. "But why walking when we can do something more magical, I mean you're a God?"

Nyx raises an eyebrow, "Well, there's a special portal that opens for occasions like this. It's how the gods travel between realms."

"A portal?" I perk up again, my curiosity reignited. "That sounds cool!" I bounce toward Nyx, ready to grab his arm and go through this magical portal together.

But as I reach out, he steps aside, just a little, enough for me to notice.

"I forgot, you're not affectionate type, huh?" I tease, trying to lighten the mood, even though it hurt my heart a little.

He raises an eyebrow, "With you yes. But I need to adapt."

"Got it," I giggle, hopping at the same time to adjust my heels.

These things will end up in the damn forest, I swear. "Lead the way to this super-duper party portal!"

Nyx smile, and we continue walking, the castle slowly shrinking behind us.

We stroll towards the edge of the forest, the breeze tousles our hair. I shoot him a mischievous grin, ready to shake things up.

"So, what's your favorite color? Or are you one of those 'I'm too cool for colors' types?" I tease, nudging him playfully.

He arches an eyebrow, a smirk tugging at the corner of his lips. "Hmm, let me think... black. Definitely black. Goes with everything, you know?"

I chuckle, enjoying his sarcastic response. "Classic choice. But what about food? Are you all about the gourmet cuisine, or do you have a secret love for human junk food?"

Nyx's lips twitch into a smirk. "Junk food, obviously. Nothing beats a good old-fashioned burger and fries."

I laugh, finding his answer unexpectedly endearing. "A man of simple tastes, I see. But what about hobbies? When you're not brooding on the edge of a floating island, crafting nightmares and terror, what do you do for fun?"

He shrugs, a hint of amusement dancing in his eyes. "I dabble in a bit of everything. Reading, stalking you,"

I raise an eyebrow, pretending to be impressed. "Stalking, huh?"

Nyx chuckles, his rough exterior softening just a bit. "Only you my dear,"

As we reach the edge of the island, I can't help but feel a warmth spreading through me. Despite his rough exterior, Nyx has a sweet spot for me, and I can't help but feel grateful for his unexpected charm.

My grumpy God.

"So," I start, my tone shifting to a more serious note, "have you ever questioned what you know about the Godsland?"

Nyx's expression grows guarded, a flicker of confusion crossing his features. "What do you mean?"

"Well, I've been doing some reading in the library," I explain, "and I've noticed some strange inconsistencies in the information about the Godsland. It's like there are pieces missing or things that just don't add up."

He tenses slightly, his jaw clenching as he avoids my gaze. ""I don't know what you're talking about, that's our story and that's what we've always been taught," he mutters, his voice tight.

I reach out to touch his arm, trying to calm the situation. He's so defensive, I'm feeling bad for pushing. "Nyx, it's okay. You don't have to pretend with me. I can tell something's bothering you."

He pulls away, his expression hardening. "This universe sucks, yeah. But it is what it is. Drop it, Aurora."

I sigh, feeling a pang of disappointment. "Okay, fine. But who taught you that? Who controls the book content? I'm just saying, it's a little weird."

We walk in silence for a while, the tension between us palpable.

And not the fun one.

I can sense Nyx's reluctance to open up, and I can't help but wonder why, I'm pretty sure it's because he, already has thought about all that.

As we approach the designated spot, a shimmering portal appears, surrounded by a faint glow.

I stand before the mesmerizing oval of lights and energy, marveling at its beauty. It shimmers with a blend of colors, and a gentle hum emanates from it, tickling my senses.

I'm about to step through, Nyx stops me, his expression serious. "Aurora, you need to stay close to me," he says. "Throughout centuries, gods have had adventures with humans, it's well known. But events like this are different. Mortals are not supposed to attend."

I furrow my brows, taking in his words. "But why if it's common for human to be in the Godsland?"

Nyx sighs, "It's the way things are, darling. Mortals have their own realms and celebrations. This is meant for gods."

"So, what does that mean for me?" I ask.

"It means you stay with me," he emphasizes, his gaze unwavering. "It's important for your safety."

He cares for me.

I nod. "Okay, I'll stay with you."

Chapter 32

Aurora

)———◇◇◇◇◇———(

Going through that portal with Nyx is like diving headfirst into a whirlwind of stars and sparkles. It feels like hurtling through an entire universe in the blink of an eye.

A rollercoaster, but not the kind where you're in a cart – this is a mind-bending journey, and I can't even see myself or Nyx. It's as if our bodies vanish, and only our minds are racing through this vibrant tunnel of ever-changing shades.

The colors are so intense, a kaleidoscope on hyperdrive, and the sparkles are like tiny galaxies zipping past. We're not just moving fast; we're soaring at the speed of light, surrounded by an explosion of sensations and energy. The portal is a cosmic spectacle where time and space blur into a mesmerizing dance of vivid shapes and hues.

Suddenly, as I'm hurtling through the cosmic colors, I notice everything around me turning black. In front of me, a pitch-black circle is expanding fast, swallowing everything in its path.

Swallowing me.

It's getting bigger every millisecond, and before I know it, I feel all the gravity pressing down on me, like that heavy feeling when you get out of a pool with clothes on.

Next thing I know, I'm on my ass, hitting the ground, *hard.*

Ouch.

The harsh light blinds me, making me squint as I try to make sense of what just happened. The colors, the sparkles, and the wild ride through the cosmic tunnel all fade away, leaving me disoriented and trying to adjust to this new, unexpected scene. The brightness of this place just pushes a realization in my head.

It's been days in the nightmare realm, where sunlight is nowhere to be found. Sunless days.

I sit there, trying to shake off the disorientation, I feel strong hands gripping my shoulders. "Aurora, are you okay?"

I blink against the harsh light, his concern grounding me as I mumble, "Yeah, just a bit dizzy. That was a wild ride." My eyes gradually adjust, and I see Nyx's concerned expression.

He helps me up, his grip firm yet gentle. "That was the portal experience. It can be intense, especially the first time. Are you feeling alright?"

I nod, still trying to wrap my head around the sudden transition. "Yeah, just need a moment to catch my breath." The surroundings slowly come into focus, revealing a place that seems both otherworldly and strangely familiar.

I gradually focus my eyes, the world in front of me unfolds like a breathtaking painting. We're standing in a vast golden field, with green grass bathed in the warm glow of sunlight.

The sky is a clear canvas, a perfect blue expanse stretching above. Every blade of grass beneath my feet seems to dance in the gentle breeze, and the air carries a sweet scent of blooming flowers.

The most beautiful place I've ever seen.

In the distance, there are magnificent structures, gleaming in perle-white and gold against the vibrant landscape. They stand tall and strong.

Laughter drifts through the air, a joyous symphony that seems to be carried by the very breeze itself.

I smile, looking at the scene before my eyes.

"Paradise," I murmur to myself.

In the corner of my eyes, I catch the eye roll and sigh Nyx makes, but I choose not to tell him.

I get a fleeting view of people in the distance, their silhouettes dancing on the horizon, walking with colorful clothes, laughter trailing behind them.

The far-off melody of music adds to the enchantment, echoing from somewhere, creating a harmonious backdrop to the paradise that unfolds before me.

Nyx observes my wide-eyed wonder at the paradise around us, a hint of annoyance in his eyes. "Alright, enough with the daydreaming," he says.

I snap out, a sheepish grin forming on my face. "Oops, got a bit carried away there. But seriously, Nyx, this place is incredible! How can you not be in awe?"

He chuckles, "I've seen it many times, Aurora. Now, let's get moving. The party awaits, and I don't want to be late nor spend my entire day here." His tone is focused as he starts leading the way towards the distant white and gold buildings.

We walk, I can't help but smile, I miss my friends, my job, and all of that.

But the atmosphere here is charged with a lively energy, with happiness and love. And I'm feeling good.

I'm almost tempted to escape from Nyx, hide somewhere here, and stay. "Why don't you seem happier to be here? It's such a nice place?" I ask Nyx.

"Because, if I let myself hope and have fun, it'll be harder to let go at the end of the day," he replies, cold, so cold. "Stop with your annoying questions, remember, no wandering off. Stick close and stay out of trouble."

Chapter 33

Aurora

We stroll through the radiant streets of paradise; Nyx and I are surrounded by an aura of pure serenity. The buildings gleam with a pristine white brilliance, reflecting the golden sunlight that bathes the entire realm.

This place.

"Isn't it too sunny here?" Nyx remarks, his voice filled with sarcasm as he gazes at me with a wink.

I nod in agreement, my eyes wide with wonder. "But it's incredible, Nyx. I've never seen anything like it."

He smiles, a rare sight that warms my heart. "I'm glad you like it. I wanted to show you the beauty of this place."

"But I'm not supposed to be here?" I ask, nervous.

"No." He simply adds.

"Won't you be in trouble?" I murmur.

"Don't worry about it. Vion won't be here and I doubt that one of the other gods will be telling on me." He responds.

We walk slowly, passing by gardens full of colorful flowers and fountains that shine with clear water.

The melody of flutes and other instruments intertwines with the laughter of people, creating a joyous symphony.

We see crowds of people dancing, their movements graceful and fluid as they twirl and sway to the rhythm of the music. Some are gathered around tables, feasting on delicious-looking foods and clinking glasses filled with shimmering drinks.

The atmosphere is electric, alive with the energy of celebration. Everywhere I look, there are smiles and laughter, as souls come together to revel in the beauty of paradise. "I wish we could stay here forever," I say, admiring the beauty around us.

Nyx smiles softly, his eyes shining with love. "Don't say that to me. Because I'll need to give it to you."

I feel the heat rushing straight to my cheeks.

"This place is so… lively," I say, amazed by all the activity.

Nyx nods proudly. "It's the heart of paradise, the heart of the realm. Farther around are the houses of the souls. But it's so big it takes years to walk around."

I smile happily, feeling grateful to be here with him. But I can't stop my mind from telling me something.

Impossible to search for the family I've lost.

A figure catches my attention. A tall man, towering above the crowd, strides confidently toward us.

Wow. He's impressive.

His presence commands attention, his muscular frame and striking features drawing the gaze of those around him.

His skin is a deep shade of ebony, accentuated by long, flowing golden hair with two locks woven into braids. The man's voice booms with joy as he greets Nyx, "Nyx, my old friend! It's been too long."

His hazel eyes, warm and welcoming, shine with a hint of mischief as he approaches. He wears a crisp white tunic that drapes elegantly over his broad shoulders, adding to his imposing yet graceful appearance.

Nyx returns the embrace, a smile playing on his lips. "It's good to see you, Airos. How have you been?"

Airos chuckles heartily, "Busy as always, you know the humans, but can't complain. And who's this lovely lady by your side?"

Nyx gestures towards me with pride, "This is Aurora,"

Aion's eyes light up as he turns to me, extending a hand. "Well, welcome to paradise, Aurora. I'm Airos God of the war realm, pleased to meet you."

I shake his hand warmly, feeling welcomed by his infectious energy but he grabs my finger slowly, bringing them to his mouth, planting a kiss on my knuckles. "Thank you, Airos. It's a pleasure to meet you too."

Airos grins, his voice booming with excitement, "You two must join us for the festivities! We're celebrating the arrival of new souls today, and it's quite the party!" He starts making absolute trash dance moves and I giggle.

Oh, I love this man.

Nyx nods eagerly while rolling his eyes, "That sounds wonderful." His tone is sarcastic, and I smile at him.

Airos sweeps a lady into his arms, and she starts laughing, clearly enjoying the unexpected gesture. I watch with wide eyes, then turn to Nyx with a puzzled expression. His white smile is contagious, and he nods his head in our direction before turning with her and walking away.

"What the heck was that?" I ask, incredulous.

Nyx sighs, shaking his head slightly. "Yep. The god of war. Always the showman."

I frown, still puzzled. "But who is she," I point in the direction they've taken. "She seems to know him pretty well, but she doesn't have the little point in the ears like all of you, gods have Is she a soul?"

Nyx explains, "She's a human, like you. He probably brought her, which is why he didn't mention anything about you. I've told you, no worries."

I nod slowly, "I see. So, is this common?"

Nyx shrugs, "It happens occasionally. Airos is known to have a soft spot for humans."

Chapter 34

The cacophony of noise surrounds me, and that feels suffocating.

Fucking exhausting.

I'm not accustomed to crowds, and the overwhelming presence of so many people make me uneasy.

Usually, I come in, I greet, I walk quickly to make the rounds, and then leave. But my love wanted to explore, smell, and see.

It's been an hour since we arrived, and I've had enough. I turn around to tell Aurora that we're leaving, but when I do, she's nowhere to be found. *Fuck.*

Panic shoots through me like a bolt of lightning. *Fuck. Fuck. Fuck.*

I start walking quickly, scanning the bustling crowd for any sign of her.

My heart pounds in my chest, my mind racing with worry.

She couldn't have gone far, could she?

I push through the hordes of people, calling out her name, but she doesn't respond.

I approach an old woman who is handing out flower crowns to passersby, hoping she might have seen Aurora. "Excuse me," I say, my voice urgent. "Have you seen a beautiful blonde woman wearing a black gown around here?"

The old woman peers at me with wise eyes, her wrinkles deepening as she thinks. "Yes, yes," she says finally, nodding. "There aren't many people wearing black on Bonum Day."

"She was so sweet. She came here with little girls; they took flower crowns. But the little girls, oh, they were so excited! They chattered away in this direction." She points, her voice quivering with age.

Relief floods through me as I thank her and follow the direction she indicated.

I quicken my pace, I need to find Aurora, to make sure she's safe. My darling will need to be punished for not listening.

My heart leaps with relief as I spot Aurora in the middle of the crowd, dancing and twirling with a group of small children.

My heart, ouch.

It feels like he grows a little wider.

And it *fucking* hurts.

She's beautiful. Smiling, with her now, flowery head. Pink, yellow, blue, and lavender plants and petals.

The way she smiles at the girls like she loves them from all her heart.

She's perfect.

She's holding a drink in her hand, and I can tell from the color that it's *aurantigranum*—a potent mixture of alcohol, pomegranate, and orange.

Oh no.

I make my way through the masses of dancing bodies, my worry dissipating as I watch her laughing and enjoying herself.

But as I get closer, I see that she's already had quite a bit to drink. It's clear with the way she had let loose. *She's going to be so drunk,* I think to myself, shaking my head with a sigh.

I feel a knot of fear tighten in my stomach. What if something had happened to her? What if she had injured herself?

I curse myself for not keeping a closer eye on her, for not protecting her better.

I lean against the railing of the gazebo above the improvised dance floor, my gaze fixed on Aurora as she twirls and dances. A smile tugs at the corners of my lips, despite the knot of worry in my stomach. She looks so carefree, so alive, and for a moment, I forget about everything else.

As if on cue, Morphea's voice pierces through the tranquility of the moment. Her tone drips with attitude and sarcasm, instantly putting me on edge.

"Well, well, well, look who we have here. The mighty God of the nightmare realm, Nyx, enchanted by a mortal girl."

I grit my teeth, suppressing the urge to snap back at her. Instead, I force myself to remain calm, though my anger simmers beneath the surface.

"What do you want, Morphea?"

"Oh, just curious about your little mortal plaything. She seems quite... captivating."

Her long, black hair cascades down her back like a waterfall of shadows, swaying with each graceful movement. She may be the Goddess of the reverie realm, but she looks like a fucking nightmare.

Her eyes, pitch black like the depths of the night, hold my gaze for a second and I want to throw her onto the damn lake nearby.

I shoot Morphea a sharp glance, my irritation growing by the second.

"Aurora is not a plaything. She's a person, with her own thoughts and feelings." I grumble.

"Of course, of course. But what is it about her that has you so entranced? Surely, there are plenty of mortals to choose from." She chuckles.

I clench my jaw, struggling to keep my temper in check. Morphea's mocking tone only serves to fuel my anger.

"Aurora is different. She's... special. And she doesn't deserve your judgment. Stay away from her you vile snake."

She raises an eyebrow "Oh, I see cousin. So, she's special, is she? How intriguing."

I resist the urge to lunge at Morphea, knowing it would only escalate the situation. Instead, I take a deep breath, trying to calm my nerves.

"Just stay out of it, Morphea. Aurora is off-limits. And for someone casting enchanting unicorns and happy thoughts you are really... Not a nice person."

She smirks "Oh, don't worry, Nyx. I'll be watching. And who knows? Maybe I'll find out just what makes this mortal girl so special after all."

With that, Morphea saunters off, leaving me seething with frustration and uncertainty.

I watch her disappear into the crowd, her pristine white gown, waving around her like a cloud.

Despite our past together when we were kids, I can't shake the feeling of unease whenever Morphea is nearby.

When it was time for us to take our thrones, we spoke of our dream realms. We were young, still hopeful about our future.

She longed for the nightmare, while I yearned for the Reveries. But Vion had other plans, and we were thrust into roles we never desired.

To everyone else, Morphea may appear pleasant and amiable, but I see through the facade. There's a darkness lurking beneath her serene exterior, a shadow that taints every interaction.

I can sense it, feel it creeping around her like a suffocating fog, and it fills me with suspicion.

I've learned to be wary of Morphea, to keep my guard up whenever she's around. There's something about her that sets my instincts on edge, a gut feeling that tells me to tread carefully in her presence.

And as much as I try to ignore it, I know better than to underestimate the darkness that resides within her.

Chapter 35

Aurora

I dance under the pretty lights, I dance with my lungs burning, *I dance.*

But everything starts to blur. This drink tastes so good, but it's making me *really, really* drunk. I don't know what they put in it, but I want another one.

I'm bouncing on the wood floor under me, moving around and having fun. But my feet are starting to hurt.

I kick off my shoes and throw them in a bush.

Told ya, heels.

The little girls around me are laughing and bouncing. Feeling happy and carefree.

And they are.

But the more I dance, the dizzier I get. My head spins, and I stumble over my own feet.

I straighten up, laughing, and raise my arms in the air, dancing to the sound of the instruments and smiling at the other inhabitants of this magnificent realm.

I keep swaying, trying to ignore the way my eyes don't wink as quickly as usual. But even with all the fun I have my head keeps yelling at me, '*where's Nyx.*'

Wasn't he supposed to be here with me? Was I supposed to stay close to him?

Fuck. I don't remember.

I look around, feeling a little worried.

He'll be soooooo mad.

I twirl unsteadily on my feet and I'm starting to fall but a strong pair of hands grabs my arm and spins me around.

"Aurora," Nyx's voice comes out gruffly, tinged with annoyance. "What do you think you're doing? Running off like that?"

I blink up at him, trying to focus through the haze of alcohol. "Nyx?" I slur, my words slightly slurred. "I was just having fun, dancing." I smiled.

He lets out an exasperated sigh, his grip on my wrist tightening slightly. "You're drunk," he states bluntly. "And you disappeared without telling me. Do you have any idea how worried I was?"

I try to protest, but my words come out jumbled and nonsensical. "I'm fine," I mumble, trying to push away his concern. "Just let me dance."

But he's having none of it. "You've danced enough," he says firmly, his tone brooking no argument. "It's time to go home."

Home.

I pout, feeling stubborn and annoyed at being told what to do. "I don't want to go home," I protest weakly, but Nyx doesn't budge.

Another song starts, the rhythm pulsating through my body, and I feel a surge of sensuality wash over me. The music seems to draw me closer to Nyx's body, and I can't help but be aware of how drop-dead gorgeous he is.

Closing the distance between us, I press my body against his, feeling the heat emanating from his skin. My movements become more fluid, more sensual as I sway to the rhythm of the music, my eyes locked on his.

"What are you doing?" He asked.

I watch the way his eyes darken with desire, the way his lips part slightly as he gazes back at me.

With a boldness fueled by the alcohol coursing through my veins, I lean in closer, grabbing with my hands his pec until my nails almost dig into the flesh.

I grind against him, the music pulsing through my flesh as I lose myself in the rhythm. In the distance, a loud voice erupts with laughter, shouting, "Oh shit, Nyx on the dance floor!"

I turn my head and catch a glimpse of Airos, his fist pumping in the air as he dances like a madman. I can't help but burst out laughing.

In that moment of distraction, Nyx seizes the opportunity to pull me into his arms, his warm breath tickling my ear as he murmurs, "Look what you've done to me."

I feel the hard length of his erection pressing against my thigh. "I'll take you somewhere, my dear." He adds.

He hugs me tightly, and in a small cloud of usual dust, he teleports us.

My feet touch down in a large space, one big room. There's velvety gold sofas and towering columns everywhere. The light is dim, which is weird compared to the hot sun outside. But what shocks me the most is the sounds and the sights.

What in the…

There are tons of naked God, having an orgy in here.

It's a lot to take in.

I stand there, feeling overwhelmed. I don't know where to look. There are penises, boobs, drool, leash, sound of flesh clapping and moaning everywhere I drop my eyes.

This is not what I expected at all.

I glance at Nyx, hoping for some guidance, but he seems unfazed.

Instead, he's scanning the room with a cool expression.

Chapter 36

Aurora

I tug nervously at the hem of my collar, suddenly feeling very self-conscious. I thought we were just going to a party, not some... *orgy* with soft and sensual modern, human music playing loud all around us.

Nyx senses my discomfort and places a comforting hand on my shoulder. "Are you okay?" he asks softly, his voice barely audible over the euphoric sounds of the room.

I shake my head, up and down, left and right, unable to find the words to express how I'm feeling. "I just... I didn't expect this, an orgy, the music." I manage to mumble, my cheeks flushing with embarrassment.

He nods and pulls me closer to him. "We love to steal things from the human realm. Their women too. We don't have to stay if you're not comfortable," he reassures me, his touch grounding me.

I take a deep breath, trying to steady my racing heart. I see beautiful people walking past us, fucking and kissing.

It makes me feel strange inside, a warmth spreading through me. I cross my legs, chasing the relief that has started burning in my core.

I think I want to stay.

The air is filled with sounds of pleasure, people moaning and sighing. "You like watching this?" He chuckles.

I face him.

"You?" I retort.

"I've never participated. But yes. I love watching." He sincerely answers.

I hear one woman's loud moans above the others, and it grabs my attention. She sounds really into it.

I wipe my head to the side and catch her eyes. A beautiful woman, her porcelain skin red where two men slap her on the butt.

Her long blond hair in a knot around an imposing man's fist in front of her.

Her soft brown gaze old mine, but her mouth is wrapping around a dick, on all four, bouncing with the movement the one fucking her in the ass makes.

My mouth slightly opens, and a breath gets caught at my lips.

"Seems to like it too, darling." The lips of Nyx graze my ear lobe and my entire body shivers.

The alcohol I drank made everything feel fuzzy and intense. I turn to Nyx and whisper, "I didn't know Gods did... this."

He looks at me, amused. "We don't usually talk about it," he says. "This woman you were looking for, it's Mora the Goddess of the nature realm."

I nod, feeling a lump in my throat. I look at his eyes with a fierce desire that takes over me, making my heart race and my skin tingle. The blood running in my veins, turning into fire.

I've never been this wet and hot in all my life. Seeing his excitement, almost breaking his pants. I can't resist anymore.

With a newfound confidence, I step back, locking eyes with him and giving him a sultry smile. He seems surprised, but I can tell he's also turned on.

Feeling bold, I reach the neckline of my dress and slowly start to remove it, swaying my hips seductively as I do.

The gown slips off completely, revealing my bare breasts in the soft light of the room. All that's left now are my black underwear.

"I don't know if I should kiss you or choke you." He growled, licking his lips.

"Choke me, my God."

Nyx's fingers wrap around my throat, sending delicious shivers in my clitoris. His lips crash against mine with a hunger that matches my own.

He breathes in my mouth, his voice a velvety melody. "You love knowing people will watch you take my dick, Aurora?" His words are bold, dripping with a raw sensuality that sets my blood on fire.

"You want me to fuck your mouth in front of all those gods?" He whispers.

I moan against his lips at the words.

YES.

"Show them, show them you got control over a God, my love." His words send a thrill through me, stirring a fearlessness that demands to be acknowledged.

I stand there, feeling powerful, I bite down on Nyx's lower lip, causing him to let out a growl.

"Fuck," he murmurs, his voice sultry.

I flash him a naughty grin, enjoying the effect I'm having on him. But before I can say anything else, he surprises me by pinching one of my nipples, making me yelp in surprise, but yearn for him to do it again.

"Ow!" I exclaim, my eyes widening.

Our little interaction catches the attention of two men and three women nearby, who start walking towards us. Feeling a rush of excitement, and without thinking too much, I take charge.

"Come on," I whisper to Nyx, pushing him by the shoulder until his back is pressed against the back of a couch.

He looks at me with glowing silver eyes.

"Take them off, god" I order, my voice dripping with confidence while pointing at his clothes.

He undresses and sits on the sofa, his body is a powerful display of raw masculinity, his hard impressive length evident for all to see, springing out of his black pants.

I take in his form, so fucking beautiful and proud.

With my chin held high, I turn to the other gods standing nearby. "Look at him," I command, pointing to Nyx. "Look at the way he will touch me, the way he will make me feel."

I gesture for them to kneel before me and touch themselves. "Feel that yearning," I taunt, my voice dripping with dominance. "That desire that you'll never be able to satisfy."

The two supreme beings obey my command, kneeling beside Nyx's legs and pleasuring themselves as I watch them squeeze their dick with satisfaction.

I look up at my *god*, his face is filled with pride and dominance, his eyes half-close, a menacing smile playing on his lips.

Turning my attention to the woman who approaches us, I glimpse at her with intensity. "Do you see this man?" I ask her, my voice low and dangerous.

The goddess nods, and I lean in to kiss her gently on the cheek. "If you do so much as breathe too close to him," I warn softly, "I'll rip your heart out."

The woman only smiles at me, the kind of smile that shows surprise and proud.

She gets it.

The deity smiles softly in Nyx's direction. "She's a keeper, nightmare god." Then kiss my hairline before leaving.

I walk towards Nyx, removing my panties, no fuck given about anyone who's watching.

In fact, loving the tang it makes in my heart.

Nyx surprises me by catching them as I throw them to the side. With a cruel smirk, he leans forward and stuffs them into the mouth of one of the kneeling men, who looks at me with wide eyes.

I'm speechless. Wet and hot.

Nyx repositions himself on the couch, his arms resting casually on each side of the back.

This confident fucker.

I smile at him.

"So jealous, my love?" he teases, his eyes gleaming.

I meet his gaze with a playful smirk. "Only of what's mine," I reply coyly.

Nyx's smirk widens, his arousal evident as he beckons me closer. "Then come fuck what's yours," he says, his voice low and enticing.

Chapter 37

My back presses against the soft cushions, and my heart races as I look at my darling, she's coming for me. My dick throbs, so hard it's painful.

Aurora sits on me, her movements sending waves of ecstasy through my entire being. She places her naked body on top of mine, spreading her legs on both sides of my legs.

She leans back, her hands resting on my knees as she grinds her wetness up and down on me. The feeling is so intense, so consuming. The sight of this pink, wet cunt spread between my dick almost makes me cum on the spot. "Fuck" I murmur.

I look at the two gods at my knees, jacking fast, mouths open, drooling for Aurora. I'm so proud to have her, to be the one touching her. She's perfect. She's mine to worship and please.

I look into her eyes, in a breathless whisper, she moans my name.

My hands find their way to her hips, guiding her movements, syncing our rhythm into the music[1] playing in the background, resonating in this big space.

Every breath, every moan, every touch is a vow that we owe each other. The pulsating sounds of pleasure echoed through the columns. The distractions surrounding me would, normally, be capable of attracting my attention but I'm fixated on her. On her mouth, her arms, her face.

Everything.

---

[1] *(Eyes on you by SWIM)*

My breath comes in short, ragged gasps as I watch her with hungry eyes.

She takes my length in her hands, her touch makes me grit my teeth. I need to control myself to let her lead this.

With a boldness that leaves me panting, she angles it at her entrance and glides down in one smooth descent, taking me in completely, not without a quick and sharp intake of hair between her tight lips.

"Ah, taking me so well," I smile at her.

She stops moving and takes the time to adjust to my size.

"Such a good girl, Aurora," I add.

I let out a low growl of satisfaction as she started moving her hips against me, her motions driving me to the brink of madness.

"You feel so fucking good," I groan.

She looks at me with dark, hungry eyes, her desire mirroring mine. "Take me, Nyx," she breathes, her voice a seductive whisper. "Take all of me, it's yours."

With a primal need driving me, I grasp her hips tightly and thrust inside her with a rough and unforgiving beat as she rides me with abandon.

I feel her body tensing beneath me, her breath coming in short, as she nears the peak of her climax.

With a final, desperate cry, we both shatter into oblivion, our bodies pulsing with the intensity of our release.

Aurora drops her head onto my shoulder, I nuzzle my nose into the crook of her neck, savoring the smell of her sweaty skin. We remain still until a sudden sound of clapping hands breaks the silence.

I stretch my head back to see Airos standing there, his hands applause together with a broad smile on his face. "Well, that was quite the show, my friends," he exclaims, his voice filled with amusement.

Aurora lifts her head, a hint of curiosity in her eyes as she gazes at Aion. "Oh…" she says, clearly uncomfortable now.

Airos nods, his smile widening. "It was beautiful, man. I wanted to join but this old Nyx probably wouldn't have let me." He winks at her.

I roll my eyes.

"But now, if you'll excuse me, I must be on my way. I have matters to attend to in my realm, and my own human to fuck." He adds with his usually charming smile.

I glance at Aurora, then back at Airos, nodding in understanding. "Of course," I say.

The god of war smile falters slightly as he looks at me, his expression serious. "Actually, Nyx, I was hoping we could have a word in private before I go," he says, his tone turning somber. "There is something we need to discuss."

I exchange a glance in my dear directions, a flicker of concern passing between us. "Of course," I reply, standing up from the couch. I make sure to hold Aurora's body close to mine to keep her intimacy while dropping her on the couch, I know she just made a *fucking*, *beautiful*, show, but still.

She feels tense right now.

With a glance down at her forms I focus on the thought of covering her.

With that, a simple, black bathrobe slowly materializes on her.

"I won't be long, darling," I murmur to her.

I rise, my nakedness a proof of my confidence, I really don't give two fucks.

I approach Airos without hesitation. His large hand land on my back, guiding me behind a column. "Aurora," He begins, his voice tainted with admiration. "She's quite remarkable."

At the mention of my woman, my mood shifts imperceptibly, and Airos notices, offering a light chuckle. "Easy, my friend. I'm not here to compete for her affections. It seems tall and skinny dark man is her type." He laughs.

I'm not skinny, but next to the god of war, built and board like an ox, I might seem more slender. But not *skinny*.

"I've talked with Morphea. You know, we're accustomed to her dramatics. But, man, she was frantic, possessed, downright insane," he adds, his expression grave. "She felt different. There was an edge to her. Yapping about this old ass prophecy I don't even remember. She was mentioning Aurora here and there and I was feeling really uncomfortable, so I left and looked for you. I'm a be honest, I didn't understand a single word she said, but watch your back."

"She doesn't belong here," Airos emphasizes, his voice heavy with concern.

Despite the warning, I'm resolute in my decision to keep Aurora by my side.

"Don't worry, we're leaving now anyway. And we'll not come to the next celebration."

"Wait, you're planning on keeping her until then?" He speaks, surprise.

I smile at him. I don't want to talk anymore. I just want to go home.

"Be vigilant," he advises. "She's human, and you're not. It's a delicate balance."

"I know. But you big ass head don't remember the prophecy she mentioned?" I ask.

He nodded in the negative, his head moving from left to right. "Just don't say I didn't warn you.

Anyway, I'm heading back to my realm now. It was good seeing you both."

I extend a hand to him, "Likewise. Take care, Airos."

He grabs my hand but, he pulls me abruptly, and my bare skin crashes against him. He wraps his arms around me, takes my face in his hands, and plants a kiss on my lips.

A wide grin spreads across his face, he steps back and disappears. "What the fuck." I murmur-laugh, confused.

This man is a damn show, but he always has been my favorite. From all the gods, *and we are a fucking tone*, Airos is real, genuine, and always sincere.

Chapter 38

I wake up next to Aurora, her serene and naked form lying peacefully beside me, in my bed. I can't help but marvel at her beauty. She looks so angelic, her long blond hair cascading over the silk pillow.

The memory of yesterday's celebration lingers in my mind, the joyful chaos of Aurora dancing now replaced by the quiet fear taking hold of me about what Airos told me.

His words echo in my mind. He spoke of his unease, his suspicions about Morphea. But it doesn't quite add up.

How could Morphea, bound to her realm like the rest of us, be a source of concern?

I furrow my brow, trying to make sense of it all as I gently caress Aurora's side, feeling the warmth of her skin beneath my touch.

It's moments like these, with my darling beside me, that I find peace.

Yet, today the uncertainty lingers.

What secrets lie beneath the surface of our world, and what role does Morphea truly play in all of this? I need to find this damn prophecy to truly understand what is going on.

"I hope you were there," I whisper to the ceiling. Hoping my mom could hear me in the Universe of Repose.

I swing my legs out of bed, feeling the chill of the room against me as I rise. Making my way across the floor, I grab a pair of pants and slip them on, the fabric brushing against my legs.

Deciding to forgo a shirt, I feel the need to go take some air before she wakes up. My curious little adventurer will probably have way too much energy and questions when she opens her eyes.

I step out of the room, gently closing the door behind me to avoid waking Aurora.

Exiting into the open air, I take in a deep breath, the scent of dew and greenery filling my lungs. The day is peaceful, the tranquility broken only by the soft rustling of the trees in the breeze.

I stretch my arm muscles above my head, groaning as I do.

I hear a strange noise coming from a line of bushes to my left.

Intrigued, I move closer, my curiosity growing with each step. I walk cautiously towards the source of the sound, my senses on high alert.

A cloud of white doves bursts out from the trees, causing me to startle and take a step back in surprise. "What the fuck?" I mutter, my heart pounding in my chest. *Fucking strange*, because I certainly didn't craft dove.

But before I can fully comprehend what's happening, a low growl reverberates from behind me.

My body tenses as I slowly turn around, only to come face to face with a horse. I damn sure know I never saw here.

It's not the gentle creature I expected, but rather an all-white unicorn with sharp, menacing teeth, drool dripping from its mouth, and blood-red eyes glaring at me.

"Fuck," I curse inwardly, realizing that it's dangerously close to the front door.

"Step back," I yell at the creature, arms outstretched in front of me to try and calm it. The unicorn lets out a toe-curling growl, its crimson haunting eyes fixed on me with an intensity that makes the message clear.

Fucking great.

Without warning, it charges in my direction, its massive teeth bared menacingly.

Instinct takes over as I roll my eyes and leap high into the air, narrowly avoiding the unicorn's deadly charge. I land gracefully on the ground with the help of my mist.

With a swift motion, I summon my abilities once more, channeling energy into my hands as I prepare to attack. The unicorn lunges again, its horn gleaming as it aims for my heart.

I sidestep its attack with agility, my movements fluid and precise.

The bastard surprises me by turning his neck at the last second and catching my forearms with his damn teeth. "FUCKER!"

I stand tall, adrenaline coursing through my veins, feeling a searing pain in my arm. Glancing down, I see blood trickling from a gash where the unicorn bites me. Anger boils inside me, fueling my determination to end this battle once and for all.

With a primal roar, I summon all my strength, feeling myself begin to float above the ground. Manifesting a sword with a flick of my wrist, I plunge towards the unicorn with fierce determination.

The clash is intense, the sound of metal against flesh echoing through the air. With each strike, I feel the weight of my anger driving me forward, pushing me to fight harder than ever before.

I need to protect my most prized possession.

And she's sleeping inside.

The unicorn fights back with equal ferocity, its powerful blows threatening to overwhelm me at every turn. But I refuse to back down, my rage propelling me forward as I press the attack.

Finally, With a powerful motion of my sword, I deliver the final blow, slicing through the unicorn's neck with a sickening sound.

Its head falls to the ground with a resounding thud. I watch as the body collapses beneath it, lifeless.

But the victory is short-lived. As the dust settles, I feel a sudden onslaught of doves descending from the sky, their wings beating frantically as they plummet to the ground around me.

"For fuck sakes,"

I raise my arms to shield myself from the onslaught, bracing for impact.

As the birds land, I observe with disbelief as both they and the unicorn, now beheaded, dissolve into thin air, leaving behind only a shimmering trail of white and gold dust.

Breathless and bewildered, I watch the remnants of the battle disappear before my eyes.

"Morphea," I grumble.

Chapter 39

Nyx

)———◇———(

I step into the castle, my arm throbs with a dull ache, the wound oozing crimson. But I pay it no mind as I stride into my office.

With rough hands, I search through the clutter, my tablet mounted on the wall the object of my frantic pursuit. Papers and trinkets scatter to the floor, but I don't give a damn. I need this shit yesterday. The pain in my arm is nothing, a mere inconvenience that my deity flesh will heal in a day or two. But what I cannot afford is for Aurora to see, to question, to pry.

Finally, I find what I seek—a small glass vial filled with powder oak roots. With a hand, I twist off the cap and sprinkle the fine powder over the open wound. A hiss of relief escapes my lips as the flesh knits together, the wound vanishing before my eyes.

It's a temporary fix, a Band-Aid over a deeper wound. But for now, it will suffice. I cannot let Aurora see it, otherwise, she'll get scared, and I'll have to reassure her even though I myself don't understand how everything that just happened is possible.

So, I'll hide my pain, behind a mask of cold indifference.

She's in danger.

And I'll not let that pass, I'm pretty sure the attack was for her and not me. I was at the right place at the right moment to prevent this vile beast to enter and kill us both in our sleep.

I'm also pretty confident that the dove was some spy. And that Morphea knows everything that happened. She will try again.

Do I send word to Vion? Do I seek his help?

I slowly run a hand through my hair as I slump heavily into my chair. "Fuck," This asshole of a King is never there for us.

I rise from my chair, a heaviness settling in my chest as I realize that this is just the beginning. The attack won't cease, and I must reach out to Vion, no matter how long it takes. Gathering information about the prophecy becomes imperative, and I must protect Aurora without her ever suspecting a thing.

I make my way to my room, where Aurora lies sleeping, oblivious to the chaos that has unfolded. I smile, but a pang of sadness grips me as I watch her peaceful form.

She's innocent in all of this, and yet she's inevitably entwined in the dangers that lurk around us. A single tear escapes my eye, trailing down my cheek and landing softly on my lips. I reach up, touching it hesitantly, a realization dawning upon me.

It's the first time I've cried since childhood. But there's no room for sentimentality now. I must do what is necessary to protect her, even if it means sacrificing everything I hold dear.

Chapter 40

Aurora

One week later

Sitting alone in the guest room, I feel as though I've been burdened with a weighty load over the past week.

I feel like shit.

It's been seven days since Nyx left me alone. Abandoning me, and I don't know why.

One morning. Without notice, I woke up alone and looked for him. Until I realized he was in his office, door closed and not responding. But I could hear him do his things on the other side of this damn door.

I've tried everything to get his attention – knocking, calling out, even pleading – but nothing.

Each day without him feels like forever. I wait for any sign that he still cares, but the silence behind the door is overwhelming. I'm starting to feel really sad and angry.

What did I do?

I'm alone here, with nothing to do except roam the forest, play with the insects, and look at the green sky. I thought I was able to stay with him, that I finally found what I was looking for, and that I could forget my past.

He made me believe that.

I was a damn fool.

I keep replaying our last moments together, wondering what I did wrong.

Did I upset him? Did I make him mad? These thoughts keep bothering me.

I don't know how much longer I can handle this. More than ever, I want to talk with Meya, I want to see the smiles on the faces of the people coming into the bakery every day.

I sit cross-legged on the floor, flipping through the pages of a large book about plants and flowers of the nightmare realm when bubbles begin to appear around me.

It's *déjà vu*, but this time there's no charm to it.

Ok. They're still cute. But I'm too mad to care.

I hear Nyx's husky voice behind me, "Sorry,"

I turn to face him, feeling a mix of relief and frustration. He's towering beside my bed, wearing a button-up black shirt and his usual black pants.

"Why bother knocking all the other time if you can just appear in my room like this?" I ask him, frustration evident in my voice.

"I knocked to give you privacy," he explains, his tone sincere. "Privacy?" I scoff, gesturing to the bubbles and the closed door. "You kidnapped me. You've fucked me. And you've left me alone in here for a week, Nyx."

Nyx's expression softens, and he takes a step closer, reaching out to gently touch my shoulder. "I know, and I'm sorry," he says earnestly. "I've been dealing with some things, but I should have communicated with you. It wasn't fair to leave you in the dark like that."

I sense a surge of frustration and hurt boiling up inside me, but I push it aside for now. "What things?" I ask, my voice trembling slightly. "Why couldn't you just talk to me about it?"

Nyx sighs, running a hand through his hair. "It's complicated," he admits, his gaze flickering away from mine. "Airos Told me Morphea was weird. Yapping about an old prophecy after seeing you. He told me to be careful."

He hesitates for a moment, it makes me unsure whether I can trust him again so easily. After all, this whole situation is ridiculous.

But then I see the sincerity in his ice-blue eyes, and I know that I want to believe him. "Okay," I say softly, nodding. "What is this…prophecy?"

Nyx sits on the floor in front of me, and I can't help but find the sight funny. A God, beautiful and strong, sitting cross-legged like a child. It's comical, and I have to fight back a laugh. But I hold it in as he brushes a blond lock out of my face.

"When waters turn green and flesh meets light, the powerful one will rise, casting shadows of pain onto the Godsland." He speaks.

I gasp out a sarcastic laugh. "Seriously? That's nonsense. What does this have to do with me?" I say, disbelief coloring my voice.

Nyx chuckles, nodding in agreement. "Indeed, baby, it does seem rather far-fetched," he replies. "But let's not dwell on it too much." His eyes darken, his voice now low and angry.

I perceive the frustration reflected in his eyes and reflexively reach out, gently placing my hand on his knee. Leaning in closer to him, I gently kiss his lips, savoring the warmth of his tongue as it pushes its way between my parted lips.

We break apart slightly, Nyx closes his eyes, and whispers against my lips, "Why are you trying to be someone else in the human realm?"

Confused, I take his face in my hands, pleading silently for him to look at me. "I don't understand," I confess, my voice barely audible. "What do you mean, someone else?"

He nods solemnly, his gaze unwavering. "I've seen you, Aurora," he mumbles, his voice soft yet filled with conviction. "I've watched you in your moments of sadness, your moments of guilt. I've seen you put on that fake smile for others, pretending that everything is okay."

His words sink in, and a lump forms in my throat. It's unsettling to think that he's been observing me without my knowledge, but at the same time, there's a strange comfort in knowing that he's seen the real me – the me that I hide from the world.

"Here, with me," he continues, his tone gentle yet firm, his face still close to mine, our breath mixing together. "You're different. You're more yourself, less this persona you've created."

With Nyx, I can be myself, unapologetically and authentically. And for that, I'm grateful.

"After everything fell apart, I tried to vanish. The pain was too much, and I just wanted to disappear, to become nothing. But for some reason, I couldn't bring myself to leave. So, I tried to look happy." I confess.

"That's where you're wrong, my dear. You thought you wanted to disappear. But all you really wanted was to be found."

We lock eyes, and I'm left speechless. His words hit home, and I can't deny the truth in them.

Chapter 41

I can see all her thoughts are spiraling just looking in her eyes. Without another word, I pull back and rise to my feet abruptly. "Go wash yourself," I say, my voice firm. "Then meet me in the living room. I have a surprise for you." I smile falsely.

I need to

Aurora gets up, confusion and curiosity tainting her features, but she still smiles at me softly.

Fuck she's beautiful when she smiles.

"What surprise?" she asks.

Always mine.

"You'll see," I reply, unable to suppress a grin of my own. "Now take these clothes off and wash yourself."

I watch as Aurora's smile grows wider, her sky-blue eyes sparkling with anticipation. She starts to dance seductively in front of me, and I feel the heat going to my groin.

She's perfect, and at this moment, I realize just how much I love her.

This is what love feels like.

But I need to.

Closing the distance between us, I help her remove her loose shirt, revealing her breasts, her pink nipple already peaking. I lick my lips with a low growl escaping me.

My fingers linger on her skin, tracing the curves of her body as she shivers beneath my touch. "Go on, take a bath," I say smoothly, trying to control my need for her.

She looks up at me with a playful glint in her eyes. "Do you want to come with me?" she asks, her voice teasing.

I hesitate for a moment, torn between the desire to join her and the necessity to keep my distance. "I... I can't," I finally manage to say, my voice strained. "I have something to take care of first."

That's bullshit.

But she needs to think it's true.

Aurora pouts playfully, her disappointment evident in her expression. "Fine," she says, her tone laced with mock indignation. "But don't take too long, or I might just start without you."

I chuckle softly at her teasing. "I won't be long," I promise, giving her a lingering look.

Aurora starts walking backward toward the bath, her nakedness impossible for me not to look. I can't tear my eyes away. "You're so enticing," I murmur my desire for her evident in my voice.

She turns on the water, the sound echoing in the room, and begins to caress her breasts with a seductive grace. "Fuck," My body reacts instantly, a primal urge coursing through me. "Aurora," I growl, my frustration evident as she teases me.

With a playful smirk, she meets my gaze, relishing in the power she holds over me. "What's wrong, my love?" she taunts, her touch driving me to the brink of madness. "Can't handle a little anticipation?"

I struggle to maintain my composure.

She pinches her nipple, closing her eyes and emitting a soft moan. Her movements, the way she closes her legs tightly, seeking friction, kindle a blaze inside me that I battle to restrain.

Adjusting my length in my pants, I force my face to look more serious. "Aurora, stop." I menace.

"No." She replies.

I reach my breaking point. I stride forward, my hands grasping her breasts and her ass with a hunger that betrays my inner fucking trouble.

My lips find her face, her neck, nipping at the delicate skin as if seeking solace in her touch.

With urgency, I lift her and guide her into the bath, but I remain kneeling beside it, unable to tear myself away. My voice is thick with emotion as I speak, my hands trembling as I reach out to touch her.

"Gods, Aurora," I whisper hoarsely, my heart heavy with unspoken words. "You've driven me to madness. I'll never be the same."

Despite the passion that burns between us, there's an undeniable sadness in my eyes, I feel it, a yearning that I struggle to transform in words.

I can't.

Instead, I express it through my actions, my touch, my unwavering presence beside her, silently revealing the depth of my heartache.

Her concern is evident as she looks at me, her eyes searching mine for answers. "Nyx, what's wrong?" she asks, her voice soft and filled with worry.

"I need to go," I say, emotionless.

I need to.

"I'll wait for you in the living room." With a heavy heart, I turn away from her and make my way out of the bathroom, leaving her alone with her thoughts.

Chapter 42

Aurora

I step out of the bath, the warmth of the water still clinging to my skin. I'm confused, frustrated, and hurt. Something is not right.

Nyx's sudden appearance after a week of silence only to disappear again has left me reeling. I don't understand his actions or his intentions.

Why would he ignore me for so long, only to show up mysteriously and then leave me alone once more, naked, and vulnerable in the bath?

I know he wanted me. I've seen the hard bulge in his pants, in hungry eyes, and felt the heat of his touch. So why would he leave me like this, without a word or an explanation?

I towel off and slip into a robe. As I approach the bed, my eyes catch sight of a pile of clothes that weren't there before.

Curiosity tugs at me, urging me to investigate further. I lean in closer, my breath catching in my throat, shock coursing through every fiber of my being.

Before me lies a simple ensemble of clothing - plain blue jeans, a panty, a bra, and a white t-shirt, accompanied by a pair of shoes.

The difference between these plain clothes and the beautiful dresses Nyx usually gives me is surprising and strange. Damn ugly, compared to the long, floaty, enchanted gown with laces and ornament.

There's definitely something not right about this.

I reach for the clothes, my hands shaking a little.

As I suspect that something is amiss, I slip on the clothes and glance over my shoulder to ensure that I am indeed alone. I delicately lift the corner of my mattress and take the pages of books I've kept hidden, folding them before placing them in my pants pocket.

I head to the living room, my mind still spiraling with questions and doubts. What does Nyx want from me? Why does he keep pushing me away and then pulling me back in? And where does that leave us now?

When I see Nyx sitting on a bench in the entryway, his expression unreadable, frustration and anger boil up inside me. I want to demand answers, to make him explain himself.

I stand in the middle of the room, my hands on my hips, glaring at Nyx. "What is going on?" I demand, my voice sharp with anger. "You disappear for a week, then show up out of nowhere, and now you leave me alone again with these... these clothes? I deserve an explanation!"

Nyx rises slowly, his movements lacking the tenderness I once knew. He approaches me, his gaze now icy and distant, and my heart sinks with a gut-wrenching fear.

"I don't want you anymore," he declares callously, his words slicing through me like a blade. "I'm bored." He smiles.

My head spins as his mean words sink in. How could he just throw me away like an old toy?

"What do you mean?" I stammer, my voice trembling with disbelief. "After everything..."

But his laughter cuts me off, mocking and devoid of remorse. "You were never more than a distraction," he sneers, his words a cruel twist of the knife. "Just a plaything to pass the time."

Tears fill my eyes as I try to understand how much he hurt me. All the nice things he said and did were just lies to trick me. "I thought..." I choke on my words, the pain in my chest unbearable. "I thought you cared..."

But his indifference crushes me, leaving me hollow and broken. "I never cared, I lied," he spits, his tone laced with disdain. "You were nothing to me."

His rejection feels like a punch right in my heart, a hand grabbing and taking away all my hopes and love.

I was just a piece in his game, and I never had a chance to win.

This was all a lie.

Tears stream down my cheeks, blurring my vision as I struggle to stay standing. The pain in my chest is overwhelming, like a physical weight pressing down on me, making it hard to breathe.

For the first time in front of him, I break down completely, my knees buckling beneath me as I collapse to the floor. The sobs wracked my body, each one feeling like another blow to my already shattered heart. It hurts so much, so deep.

It hurt.

All the love I had for him, all the dreams of a future together, they're all gone now, replaced by a crushing emptiness. How could he be so cruel?

But even as I ask myself these questions, I know there are no answers. He's made his choice.

He sinks to my level, his silver eyes empty of emotions as he reaches out to touch my face. Gently, he wipes away the tears streaming down my cheeks, his touch agonizing.

"Don't you dare," he whispers. But his words just make me hurt more. I can feel his pain too, just as much as my own. I know it's there.

It's like we're both feeling the same thing for a moment, but it doesn't change anything.

I stare into his eyes, searching desperately for some sign of reassurance, some glimmer of hope to hold onto. But all I find is emptiness, a void where once there was warmth and love. Everything around me starts to fade away into swirling darkness.

"Please," I cry out, tears streaming down my cheeks, "don't leave me alone."

The room around me starts to dissolve into a swirling, black, glittery mist.

The wind whips around me, tearing at my clothes and tossing my hair wildly. But despite my pleas, he continues to vanish before my eyes.

"No." I cry.

The last thing I see is his face, blurred and distant amidst the swirling darkness.

"NYX!"

He fades into nothingness; a single tear rolling down his cheek.

"Sleep, my dear."

Chapter 43

Aurora

)———◇———(

I wake up feeling confused, looking around. The walls are colorful, and decorated with paintings and funny things. Sunlight comes in through the windows.

I'm home.

Sitting up, I take in the warmth of the sunlight and the cozy atmosphere of my living room. Feeling sad and confused, I call out for Nyx, hoping he'll appear and make sense of everything.

"Nyx, please."

But there's no answer, just the silence of my empty home.

My phone suddenly starts ringing, startling me.

I glance over at the side table and see my cell phone lying there plugged into its charger.

I stretch out an arm and grab it, using my other hand to massage my forehead.

It's full of missed calls and text messages from Meya, overwhelming me with urgency and dread.

My hands start to shake as I check the date. "What the hell," I mutter to myself, realizing it's been a week since Nyx kidnapped me.

I know I stayed *way* longer than that in the nightmare realm. I scratch my head and remember him explaining the time difference between our realms.

I hesitantly tap on the call button, my heart pounding as I bring the phone to my ear. I wait for her to say something but it's silent. "Hello?" I say, my voice trembling slightly. "Meya?" I ask, my voice.

There's a brief pause on the other end of the line before Meya's voice comes through, sharp and filled with anger. "Where the fuck have you been, Aurora?" she demands. "You disappeared without a word for a whole week. I've been worried sick!"

I flinch at her harsh tone, feeling a pang of guilt wash over me. "I-I'm sorry, Meya," I stammer, struggling to find the right words to explain. She won't understand and she will put me through a psychiatric hospital.

I swallow hard, trying to find the words to calm Meya's anger. "I'm sorry. I was really sick. I couldn't even get out of bed," I say.

But Meya doesn't seem satisfied with my explanation. "Sick? You better have been sitting on your toilet dying for me to forgive the fact that you didn't at least text me," she snaps, her tone biting with sarcasm. "I was worried about you! I even knock on your damn door. I was about to send the police today."

I flinch at her words, feeling guilty. Because I was good. I wanted to stay there. "I know, I'm sorry," I repeat, my voice barely above a whisper. "I... I wasn't thinking clearly. I don't know what happened."

Meya's anger doesn't slacken as she continues to vent her frustration, her words like daggers piercing through my already fragile heart. "Listen, Aurora," she says firmly. "I want a key to your place. Now. This is non-negotiable. I refuse to sit around worrying about you like this ever again."

"Okay," I say softly. "I'll get you a key. I promise."

Meya seems to calm slightly at my compliance, but there's still a hint of frustration in her voice as she responds. "Good, because I'm fucking angry with you, Aurora. And you better believe we're going to have a serious talk about this when I see you. But do you need me to bring you to the ER or something?"

"Meya," I say, my voice wavering slightly. "I'm okay now, really. I don't need to go to the ER or anything."

There's a moment of silence on the other end of the line before Meya responds. "Are you sure?" she asks, genuine concern in her voice.

I nod, even though she can't see me. "Yeah, I'm sure. I'll be fine," I assure her, forcing a note of confidence into my voice.

I won't be.

Meya lets out a sigh, her frustration giving way to relief. "Okay, good. Just... take care of yourself, okay? And come to work tomorrow. I need you," she says, her voice tinged with sincerity.

I manage a small smile, grateful for her concern despite everything. "I will. Thanks, Meya," I say.

With that, we say our goodbyes, and I hang up the phone, feeling a weight lift off my shoulders.

It's a small comfort knowing that she's looking out for me, at last, I have one person still loving me.

Chapter 44

Aurora

One month later

It's been a whole month since I got back to my usual routine. I keep trying to tell myself that what happened was just a crazy dream, or maybe some kind of coma.

But deep down, I *know* it was real.

Every night, when I close my eyes, I find myself in the complete dark. No dreams, no nightmares. Just nothing. Each night, a part of me hopes to open my eyes in this dark forest, earing the bats and the glowing butterflies. And I start to wonder if it's Nyx's way of showing me how much he doesn't care about me.

Or if something happened to him. I have this feeling in my gut.

Even though I'm back in the real world, I can't shake the feeling that Nyx was lying.

He loves me.

During the day, I try to act normal, but inside, I'm still torn up about everything that happened. I go about my business, but it feels like I'm just going through the motions.

I miss him.

Part of me still hopes that Nyx will find a way to get back to me, to bring me back, but as time goes on, that hope starts to fade. I'm starting to accept that maybe it's never going to happen again, and it hurts more than I can say.

I enter the bakery, and I greet the familiar faces with a smile, trying to push away the lingering thoughts of him. I slip off my hoodie and glance down at the bright yellow apron tied around my waist. "I'm so ridiculous," I mumble to myself.

I grab a tray of freshly baked chocolate chip cookies, their warm aroma wafting through the bakery, and I head to the front counter to display them for customers.

A deep, masculine voice greets me. "Hello, Aurora."

I glance up and see Josh standing there, his familiar face sending a pang of annoyance through me. "Oh, it's you," I say, my tone dripping with sarcasm.

I neither forget nor forgive.

He clears his throat, shifting uncomfortably. "Hey, I, uh, wanted to talk to you about that night..."

I raise an eyebrow, crossing my arms defensively. "What, the night you were absolutely rude?"

Josh winces, running a hand through his hair. "Yeah, that one. Look, I know I messed up, but I swear I didn't mean to..."

I cut him off with a sharp gesture. "Save it, Josh. I don't want to hear your excuses."

He sighs, looking genuinely remorseful. "I just wanted to apologize, Aurora. I know I messed things up between us, and I regret it."

I roll my eyes, turning away from him to focus on arranging the cookies. "Apology not accepted."

Josh frowns, his expression pleading. "Come on, Aurora. Can't we at least talk about it?"

I shake my head, refusing to meet his gaze. "There's nothing to talk about. Josh. Just leave me alone."

He opens his mouth to say something else, but I cut him off with a dismissive wave of my hand.

Turning my back on him, I try to focus on my work, hoping he'll take the hint and leave me in peace.

I retreat into the kitchen, Meya follows me, her expression concerned. "Hey, girl. Everything's okay?"

I force a smile. "Yeah, I'm fine. Just dealing with an unwanted visitor."

Meya raises an eyebrow, glancing back towards the front of the bakery where Josh is still lingering. "Ah, I see. Mr. Drunk-Asshole is back, huh?"

I nod, feeling frustrated. "Yeah, he's trying to apologize or something. I don't know. I'm not interested."

Meya studies me for a moment, her gaze penetrating. "Maybe you should hear him out, Aurora. It might give you some closure."

I shake my head adamantly, my frustration mounting. "No way, Meya. I don't need closure from him. I've already made up my mind about him. I don't need to hear his excuses."

She sighs, placing a comforting hand on my shoulder. "I get it. But sometimes it helps to listen, you know? Just think about it."

I shrug off her hand, my annoyance growing. "I don't need to think about it. I know what I want."

Meya gives me a sympathetic look, "Maybe a dick would put a smile back on that face of yours." She adds and goes back to the front of the bakery, leaving me alone with my thoughts.

I stand in the kitchen; the thought crossing my mind like a shadow dancing on the edge of my consciousness.

No.

Maybe.

Just ounce.

I could let him dick me, laugh at his small dick, and savor my vengeance watching him leave with a walk of shame.

Move on from whatever lingering emotions still tie me to Nyx.

I'm incapable of putting on the facade I used to, and I can't shake this feeling of loneliness that clings to me like a second skin.

Josh is undeniably attractive, with his rugged good looks and easy charm. Maybe I can distract myself from feeling so empty inside.

With a heavy sigh, I make my way back to where Josh is waiting in the bakery, seated at a table with his coffee.

I approach, and he looks up at me expectantly, and I can see the hope in his eyes. I take a deep breath, steeling myself. "I'll see you at my place tonight, at eight."

Josh's face lights up with a smile, and he nods eagerly in agreement. "I'll be there," he says, his tone filled with anticipation.

With that settled, I turn away, my heart heavy with conflicting emotions.

Deep down, I know this isn't the right decision, but for now, it's the only one I can make.

Chapter 45

———————

I stand in front of the mirror, examining my reflection with uncertainty. I smooth down the fabric of the black dress that hugs my curves, its simple yet elegant design offering a contrast to my colorful clothes.

I bought it on a whim after work, drawn to its understated beauty and the way it seemed to speak to the darkness that lurks in me. In *Nyx*.

My long blonde hair cascades down my back in loose curls, framing my face in a soft halo of golden waves. I've taken extra care with my makeup today, opting for a subtle smoky eye and a bold red lip that adds a touch of confidence to my appearance.

I look at myself and wonder what tonight will be like. Will it help me feel less lonely? Or will it just make me feel even more empty inside?

Taking a deep breath, I try to push away my worries but a knock on the door interrupts my brainstorming, causing me to glance over my shoulder.

I walk to the door and open it. Standing there is Josh, looking as handsome as ever.

"Hey," he says, his voice smooth and charming. "You look amazing."

I smile and invite him in. "Thanks," As he steps inside, I can't help but notice the way his eyes linger on me.

"Wow, you really went all out," he says, nodding approvingly at my outfit. "I like it,"

I blush, feeling at his compliment. "I wanted to look nice for tonight."

He grins, stepping closer. "Well, you definitely succeeded."

I offer him a glass of wine, and he nods appreciatively, his demeanor seemingly relaxed.

I force a small smile, trying to maintain a sense of normalcy despite the unease brewing inside me.

Something's wrong.

I turn to walk towards the kitchen and feel his eyes on me, watching my every move. "Nice place you've got here, I didn't look at it the other time," he comments, attempting to make conversation.

I nod, keeping my back to him as I open the bottle of wine. "Thanks," I reply, my tone polite but distant. "I've been here for a while now." I add.

I pour the wine into the glasses, but I can't shake the feeling that something isn't right. I don't love the way he's looking at me.

This was a mistake.

Ok. Breathe, Aurora. You'll drink this glass, talk, and kick him out.

There's a tension in the air, *not the sexual kind*, that hangs between us like a heavy fog.

"Here you go," I say, turning to offer him the glass.

He takes it from me, his hand brushing against mine. I pull away instinctively, a sense of foreboding settling over me like a dark cloud.

And then, without warning, everything changes when his mouth opens, and his eyes look at the floor. "I'm so, so, sorry."

He lunges at me, his hands outstretched towards my neck.

Instinctively, I stumble back, narrowly avoiding his grasp. Adrenaline courses through my veins as I realize his intentions, and I quickly assess the situation.

Ducking under his arm, I spin around and deliver a swift kick to his abdomen. He grunts in pain, but he doesn't relent. Instead, he lashes out with surprising speed, aiming to strike me once more.

I dodge his blow, narrowly avoiding the edge of his hand as it slices through the air. With a surge of determination, I counterattack, landing a series of rapid punches to his torso. He staggers backward, momentarily stunned by the force of my assault.

Seizing the opportunity, I grab a nearby chair and swing it towards him, aiming for his head. He ducks just in time.

Despite his attempts to fight back, I refuse to let up, channeling all of my anger and frustration into each strike. With each blow, I feel a sense of empowerment, knowing that I am fighting for my life.

Finally, I see an opening—a moment of doubt in his eyes. Without hesitation, I deliver a powerful kick to his chest, sending him crashing to the ground.

He lies there, gasping for air, I stand over him, my breath ragged but my resolve unwavering.

"What the fuck," I gasp, breathless.

"You...you need to die." Josh spits. His eyes are full of disgust on me.

I put a heavy foot on his throat and grip the handle of a knife nearby on the counter, my fingers trembling with fear and anger. "What is happening, Josh? You wanted to kill me?" I demand, my voice trembling with emotion.

But instead of answering, he just laughs, his gaze fixed on the ceiling as if he's lost in some kind of delirium. "My love, I almost did it," he mutters, his words slurred and disjointed. "I'm sorry I failed."

"Stop playing games!" I shout, my patience wearing thin. "Tell me what's going on!"

But he just continues to laugh, his laughter echoing off the walls of the room like a haunting refrain. With a frustrated growl, I lunge forward, driving the knife into his shoulder with all the force I can muster until I feel the blade stop on the floor underneath him.

He cries out in pain, his body jerking in shock as blood begins to trickle down his chest.

Finally, with tears streaming down his face, he manages to choke out a single word. "Morphea," he gasps, his voice barely above a whisper.

What...

The name hangs in the air like a curse, sending a chill down my spine.

"What do you mean, Morphea?" I demand, my voice trembling with emotion.

He spits out blood, his words come out in ragged gasps, each one laced with pain. "My goddess, Morphea," he wheezes, "she's been bringing me to her realm for a long time. She's... in love... with me."

My heart sinks at his words, disbelief and horror coursing through me. "Continue," I demand. "What did I have to do in that?"

He struggles to speak through the pain, his breaths coming in shallow gasps. "She said... you're a danger... that you need to die," he manages to choke out. "Since she couldn't... take hold of you... while you slept... she sent me... to do the job."

The reality of his words hits me like a physical blow, sending a wave of nausea washing over me. Morphea, had been plotting my demise all along.

I look down at the man thrashing in pain before me, I know that I can't let him be the instrument of my destruction.

I'm done now.

With a determined grimace, I smile at him.

Chapter 46

Aurora

With a steady hand, I wrench the knife from his shoulder and plunge it into the other one, eliciting a cry of agony from him. His body convulses with pain, tears streaming down his face as he pees on the floor.

Leaning in close, I whisper, my voice low and filled with urgency, "Tell me more, and I'll make your death quicker. Pussy."

His breaths come in ragged gasps, his eyes wide with fear and desperation. "Please," he pleads, clearly realizing I'm not the defenseless girl he thought he was attacking. "I'll tell you everything. Just make it stop."

I wait patiently as he gathers his thoughts, his words tumbling out in a rush as if he's afraid he'll lose his chance to speak. "Morphea," he begins, his voice trembling with fear, "she's been watching you, waiting for the right moment to strike since Bonum Day. She sees you as a threat, a danger that needs to be eliminated for the Godsland."

Dropping my ass on my heels, I crook my head to the side, smiling at him.

I'm done hiding.

Josh continues, his words coming out in short bursts between labored breaths and blood cough. "Morphea found a way to travel between the Godsland realms. She's been trying to send her power to kill you in the nightmare realm for a week straight, but each time, that damned god of nightmare protected you."

I listen intently, my mind racing with the implications of his words. Nyx.

He was protecting me.

"And then," Josh continues, his voice growing weaker with each passing moment, "Morphea broke into his castle, looking for you. But you weren't there anymore."

I'm filled with an overwhelming sense of rage as I kick the man hard in the crotch.

"What happened to Nyx?" I scream, my voice trembling with fury.

But he can only groan in pain, unable to provide me with the answers I desperately seek.

Tears stream down my face as I struggle to contain the storm of emotions raging inside me. "Tell me!" I shout again, my voice raw with desperation.

But still, he remains silent, writhing in agony on the floor.

I refuse to give up. "Did she find the black lotus?" I yell at him.

He looks at me with small eyes, he's dying.

"What?" He murmurs.

Josh's breath stops, and he falls lifeless.

I drop to my knees, screaming with all my might.

Nyx may be gone too. Especially if she already found the black lotus.

I rise slowly from the floor, my heart pounding with determination.

Memories of my life before Nyx flooding my mind.

With a small, secretive smile playing on my lips, I whisper to myself, "It's time."

Hurrying into the bathroom, I fling open the cabinet doors, my hands shaking as I search for the somniferous.

Finally finding the small bottle, I gulp down two pills, the bitter taste lingering on my tongue. Sinking on the floor, I close my eyes and let the darkness swallow me whole.

I summon the pain, the heartache, the despair of the worst day of my life.

I remember the loss, the betrayal, the suffocating darkness that threatened to consume me. With every breath, I draw upon that pain, using it to fuel my determination to find my way back to the nightmare realm.

Behind closed eyelids, flashes of my past flicker to life, forming shapes of terror and despair. I push deeper into the darkness, willing myself to confront the nightmares that haunt me.

With one final thought echoing in my mind, I embrace the darkness, knowing that only by facing my demons head-on can I hope to find the revenge I seek.

The stormy beach stretches out before me, waves crashing violently against the shore. Above, crows circle, their harsh cries echoing in the tumultuous air. I stand at the water's edge, facing the roiling sea with a mixture of fear and determination.

Taking a deep breath, I whisper to myself, "You will not fear," steeling my resolve as I step into the water.

The waves crash against me with a force that threatens to knock me off my feet.

Ignoring the pounding of my heart, I continue forward, each step a battle against the relentless onslaught of the ocean. Soon, the sand slips away beneath my feet, and I find myself surrounded by the icy embrace of the sea.

With a shaky breath, I begin to swim, pushing myself further and further from the safety of the shore. The green and cloudy sky darkens overhead, and rain begins to pour down, mingling with the salty water.

I tilt my head back and let out a primal scream, a desperate plea for the darkness to consume me.

I submerge myself beneath the churning waves, feeling the weight of the water pressing down on me, threatening to crush me with its relentless force.

I open my mouth and gulp down a mouthful of water, the salty liquid burning my throat as I struggle to breathe.

I sink deeper into the depths, and the world around me fades away, replaced by an overwhelming sense of peace.

The pounding of my heart slows, and a strange calm is washing over me, enveloping me in its cool embrace.

At that moment, I am no longer afraid.

Because if he's still alive… He won't let me drown.

Chapter 47

)———◇◇———(

I find myself in a dark forest, surrounded by towering trees and shadows.

Nightmare realm.

I've made it.

I force myself to have a nightmare. And he saves me.

The air is thick with an eerie silence, broken only by the occasional rustle of leaves and the distant hoot of an owl. It's unsettling, but there's a strange sense of familiarity that washes over me.

In the distance, I spot a figure moving through the shadows, its form barely visible in the darkness. It draws closer, and I realize it's a little girl, her silhouette illuminated by the faint green skylights filtering through the canopy above.

She looks wet, her tear-streaked face hauntingly familiar.

"Aurora?" I whisper, the name feeling like a whisper of memory in the stillness of the forest.

It's impossible.

The girl stops in her tracks, her eyes widening in recognition before she rushes towards me, her footsteps echoing through the quiet forest.

She throws her arms around me in a tight embrace, her tears mingling with mine as we hold each other tightly.

"Thank you," She speaks softly. I look down at her, but she disappears into the darkness of the forest, leaving me alone once again, my mind racing with thoughts and memories.

"AURORA!" I yelled, wanting to know why she was thanking me. Because she shouldn't. But she's gone, nowhere to be seen now.

I once read a book I stumbled upon in Nyx's library, hidden among the dusty tomes and ancient scrolls. It spoke of humans who found themselves in the realm of nightmares, burdened by their guilt and regrets.

They were so focused on their fear, that without the help of the god they fell into a nightmare.

I took the fucking chance. And it worked.

Without wasting a moment, I start running through the forest, my heart pounding in my chest as I push myself forward.

I sprint until finally, breathless, and weary, I arrive at the familiar sight of the black lotus.

Relief floods through me as I see the black lotus still standing tall, hidden, and untouched.

"She didn't find it." This means I still have a chance.

With a determined gaze, I mutter to myself, "Now they'll feel my anger." Extending my arm, I grasp a long thorn tightly in my hand.

I bring it close to my heart and press it against my skin, screaming out in agony as the pain courses through me. The moment the thorns pierce my flesh, it feels like a thousand needles stabbing into me all at once, leaving trails of blood in their wake.

The sky above darkens, as if sensing the intensity of my agony, and strange, otherworldly sounds fill the air, echoing around me.

I collapse to my knees, my hands trembling as I try to steady myself. Behind my tightly closed eyelids, flashes of images flicker, each one more haunting than the last.

It feels like fire coursing through my veins, burning hotter with each passing moment. I feel my skin prickling and tingling as if something is stirring beneath the surface. And then, there's a searing sensation on my scalp, as if my very skull is on fire.

With a guttural cry, I reach up to clutch at my head, only to feel something sharp and pointed emerging from my skull. Horns—*my horns*—are breaking through the skin, tearing their way into the world with a relentless force.

The pain is unbearable and overwhelming, but somewhere deep within me, I know that I have to endure it. Blood starts dripping from my head to my face, mingling with my tears.

This is my path, my destiny—and I will see it through, no matter the cost.

As the pain begins to ease, the distant sound of thunder reverberates through the air. I take deep breaths, each one bringing a sense of calm and clarity to my racing mind.

Laughter bubbles up from deep within me, uncontrollable and wild.

Rising to my feet, I extend my hands to my sides, feeling the power coursing through me. With a flick of my wrist, I summon a mirror before me, watching as it materializes in the air.

Peering into the glass, I see myself.

My blond hair has grown longer, cascading down my back in unruly waves. Two black, curly horns protrude from my skull, blood dripping from their tips to the ground below.

And where once my eyes were a vibrant blue, they now burn with a fiery red intensity, evidence of the power I've just unleashed.

Taking a deep breath, I release the mirror, watching as it falls to the ground with a satisfying crash. The cacophony of crows falls silent, their eyes fixed on me as look at them taking their places on the trees.

"It's been a while." I smile at them.

With a crack of my neck from side to side, they start flying on the ground. Surrounding me, *recognizing* me.

"I am Elligan, Ancient and first Goddess of Death and War, fallen at the end of the false king, Vion" I proclaim, my voice ringing out in the echo of this realm.

"And the gods will feel my wrath."

MAKE YOUR OWN
AURANTIGRANUM
COCKTAIL

Ingredients:

1 ½ oz pomegranate juice

1 oz freshly squeezed orange juice

1 ½ oz coconut rum

½ oz peach schnapps

½ oz grenadine syrup

Ice cubes

Orange slice and maraschino cherry for garnish

Instructions:

Fill a cocktail shaker with ice cubes.

Pour in the pomegranate juice, freshly squeezed orange juice, coconut rum, peach schnapps, and grenadine syrup.

Shake well until the mixture is thoroughly chilled.

Strain the mixture into a glass filled with ice.

Garnish with an orange slice and a maraschino cherry for a delightful presentation.

Stir gently before sipping and enjoy your God's cocktail!

BY THE SAME AUTHOR

- **Say Sorry (A second chance romance novella)**
- **StepPsycho-Tangled hearts, Twisted fates Duet#1 (A dark-forbidden romance)**
- **Ruins and shadows (A enemies-to-lovers romantasy)**
- **Sleep my dear – The Godsland Book One (A dark romantasy)**

Made in the USA
Coppell, TX
27 April 2025

48758889R00208